On His Grave

M K Farrar

Published by Warwick House Press, 2019.

This is a work of fiction. Similarities to real people, places, or events are entirely coincidental.

ON HIS GRAVE

First edition. June 6, 2019.

ISBN: 978-1072489245

Written by M K Farrar.

Chapter One

"You've got to be kidding me!"

Kristen Scott stared down at the letter she'd just opened and put out a hand to support herself against her hallway wall. Her stomach dropped, and she sucked in a shaky breath.

The letter from the energy company blurred as her eyes filled with tears. How could they do this? An increase of fourteen percent on both her gas and electricity bills due to rising costs, the letter informed her. Yeah, right. As if they needed that money. Profits of billions were probably nothing to them, and here she was crying over having to find another nine pounds a month to pay for the absolute bare necessities.

She'd barely been managing to scrape by as it was. She put the heating on for an hour at night if it got really cold, but, even then, she only put it on in her son's room. She made sure Ollie got the first bath, and then she jumped into his water after him. Sometimes, if the cold had got right down to her bones, she sneaked in with him, but he'd soon be at the age where the last thing he'd want was suffering his mother naked in the bath with him. She didn't even cook food that meant the oven going on for any length of time—not that she could afford anything more exciting than pasta with a bit of grated cheese on top, or a potato she'd blasted in the microwave. Ollie got free school meals during term time, and she could last without lunch herself, but things were even harder during the holidays when she had to find three meals a day for him.

You didn't take care of those pennies, Kristen, her mother's voice tutted in her head. *What did I always say to you about taking care of those pennies?*

But she had. She'd always looked after the pennies, and the pounds as well. She didn't have any choice. But it never seemed to make any difference.

"Mummy, what's wrong?"

Kristen glanced down to see her five-year-old son staring up at her, his brown eyes—eyes so like hers—wide with worry.

She forced a smile. "Oh, nothing, sweetheart. Just stupid old bills."

His lips twisted. "Do they want more money?"

It broke her heart that he even knew she worried about how much everything cost—not that it was surprising. She felt as though every other thing that came out of her mouth was 'no, we can't afford it.'

She blinked furiously to hold back the tears. "Only a little. It'll be okay." Putting her arm around his narrow shoulders, she gave him a squeeze. "Nothing for you to worry about."

He looked at her as though he didn't believe her, and she knew she had to distract him. "Hey, shall we go and play with your Play-Doh? We can make some ugly monster."

Ollie's eyes lit up. "Yeah, I'm going to make a green snot monster!"

"Eww, that sounds disgusting."

"It is!" he enthused. "Really extra disgusting."

The boy bounded away to the dining room table where she always insisted they did messy games, and Kristen followed, pushing away the sinking in her gut. Sometimes it felt as though everything was trying to trample her down. It had been almost two years since Stephen had left, and she'd imagined things would have got better by now. But instead, things seemed even harder, especially since Stephen and his new wife had had their own baby together. The new wife—Lisa—already had a little girl of her own, the same age as Ollie, and now they had a brand-new baby together to complete their little family. Stephen was supposed to have Ollie every other weekend, but since the baby had been born, he was cancelling more often than not, leaving her to mop up the tears of their disappointed son. Though she wished she could voice her frustrations and tell Ollie how Stephen was putting the new baby before his eldest son, she managed to clamp her mouth around the words and come up with excuses instead—Daddy was poorly, or something came up with work. And she always finished up with how sorry Stephen was and how much he'd miss Ollie, even though those words had never come out of Stephen's mouth. Saying the truth of how things really were might make her feel better, but only temporarily. She knew she'd regret it as soon as the words came out of her mouth. They'd only cause Ollie pain, and that was one thing she couldn't stand.

This news about the hike in energy costs was just another kick in a long line of kickings. Her job in the office of Ollie's school wasn't enough to keep them going. Sometimes she thought she'd be better off not working at all and claiming benefits instead, but the idea made her heart sink even further. She liked being at the school, spending time with the kids and staff. The prospect of sitting at home, alone, every day was heart breaking.

No, something needed to change. She didn't know what, but she couldn't go on as they were. She felt like her life was slipping between her fingers.

The house was the one thing she'd kept from her broken marriage, though there were plenty of times she wondered if she'd have been better off to sell and take the small amount of equity in the property. At least then she'd have some money in the bank. But the fact of the matter was that their mortgage was small, and with Stephen still paying half, there was no way she'd be able to rent somewhere privately for less money. The waiting list for council properties was huge, and they wouldn't even look at her if she owned her own home. The agreement was that she and Stephen would continue to pay the mortgage together until Ollie reached eighteen or finished full time education, and then they'd sell—hopefully mortgage free—and divide the money between them.

Besides, she loved her house. It had been her home for six years now, and the idea of moving into a tiny, two-bedroom flat with no garden made her soul weep. She'd figure it out. She had to.

The weekend stretched ahead of her, trying to get through each hour until it was time to go back to bed. It was difficult to find things to do when there was no money in the bank. She took Ollie down to the park, or to ride his little second-hand bike down by the river. Sometimes, she got invites to go to one of the other mums' houses for a bite of lunch, or even a cup of tea while the boys played, and she was always inherently grateful for those kinds of invitations. When they involved paying out money—going to the zoo or taking the kids swimming—she always had to beg off with some excuse or another. The other parents in Ollie's year had given up inviting her on nights out. She always said it was because she had Ollie and couldn't afford a sitter. Truthfully, her sister, Violet, could have had him for a few hours at a push, though leaving Ollie with Violet always made Kristen nervous. But she couldn't afford the overpriced drinks and couldn't bring herself to waste money like that even if she had it. Instead, she watched their group messages they were always polite enough to include her in, even though there was never any chance of her going, seeing how much fun they were having and trying not to feel bitter about it.

"Come on, then," she told her son, forcing herself to smile and shoving the letter from the energy company into the rack containing all the other mounting bills. "Let's see who can make the most disgusting Play-Doh monster."

MONDAY MORNING FINALLY arrived. Sometimes, Kristen felt like she must be the only person who looked forward to the working week rather than being at home.

"Hey, how was your weekend?" asked Anna, the woman she shared her school office job with.

The school was small, with barely a hundred pupils on a good day. The two women managed the office between them, chasing paperwork from the parents, handling new intakes, and tallying lunch money, amongst a million other things. It was busy and sometimes stressful, and obviously the money wasn't exactly great, but it meant Kristen was able to drop off Ollie at the school's breakfast and afterschool club without any charge, and she was off at the weekends and school holidays so she was always there for him. Of course, she wished she was able to earn more, but she had to think about Ollie. His father was so unreliable these days, and she couldn't depend on her sister for childcare, so she needed something that would work around him, and this job was perfect for that.

"It was fine," she said with a tight smile, trying not to think about how she'd spent last night crying into her pillow in the hope she didn't wake Ollie.

Anna frowned at her. "Really? You seem a bit pale this morning."

Kristen knotted her hands in her hair, her elbows on the desk as she shook her head. "Oh, it's nothing. Just money stuff. Bills seem to keep creeping up all the time, and sometimes I'm not sure how I'm going to keep paying them."

"Isn't Stephen helping you out?"

"He pays the bare minimum of what the courts told him. Now he's got the new baby, he keeps saying he doesn't have spare cash for anything extra. Ollie put a hole in his school trousers at the end of last week, and I had to buy a new pair. Then I got a letter from the energy company to say they were putting the bills up. I know it doesn't seem like much, but all these little things keep adding up."

Anna gave her a sympathetic smile, but Kristen knew she didn't really understand. Anna's husband worked as someone important in a big firm and brought in a more than decent wage. Anna said they needed the money from her job, but she had no idea what it was really like to need money. They took several foreign holidays a year, and Anna's children did pony club at the weekend. Anna's blonde hair was always shiny and freshly cut, her nails professionally manicured, her clothes and beauty products top of the line. She didn't know how it felt to feed your child pasta three days in a row because you literally couldn't afford anything else.

Anna pursed her pretty lips and tapped her pencil against them. "Your house is a three bed, isn't it?"

"Yes, that's right."

"What about getting a lodger?"

Kristen wrinkled her nose. "Yeah, I've thought about it. The idea of giving some stranger access to my home is worrying, though. How do I know they won't be a complete creep? I've got Ollie to think about, and I don't want to bring a stranger into the house if they might turn out to be a weirdo."

"I know what you mean. What about if the person is already vetted, though?"

She shook her head. "I don't trust letting agencies, if that's what you mean."

"No, it isn't. I'm thinking about foreign students. I know the university is always looking for housing near to town."

"Foreign students? You mean teenagers?"

She shrugged. "They have teenagers, sure, but they also look for people who are willing to house mature students for longer periods. I think they're still young, but they're technically adults, and they're really here to study, so it's not like they're out partying or anything like that."

Kristen twisted her lips. "I don't know. It would feel strange having someone else living in the house."

"Well, have a think about it. It's good money. I think you can get two hundred pound a week, if you feed them, too, and it's tax free."

Her mouth dropped. "Seriously?"

"Yep, seriously."

The idea of an extra two hundred pounds a week was mind-boggling. It would make a massive difference to her—to Ollie, too. She could stop saying she couldn't afford things every time he asked for a new toy, or to go swimming, or to soft play. A foreign student wouldn't be as bad as having a random stranger in the house. They wouldn't have a ton of friends and other family around, so they would be forced to become a part of hers, in a way. Something about the idea resonated with her. She didn't want a stranger living in her home, but having someone who might feel like a part of the family, and would share meals with them, felt right. She had been lonely since Stephen left, and having a five-year-old around wasn't the same as another adult. She missed having someone to talk to, and a foreign student would want to talk to her, wouldn't they? They'd appreciate being able to practise their English.

Kristen got on with the day's jobs. There was a residential coming up for years five and six, and at least half the parents hadn't filled in the paperwork or paid the final instalment yet. She hated chasing other parents for money—always putting herself in the position of parents who might be making excuses about why they hadn't paid yet, when the truth was that they were simply too embarrassed to admit they couldn't afford it. There were schemes to help people on low incomes pay, but everyone was too proud to apply for them, unless they were desperate. At lunch time, she waved to Ollie as he went into the hall to eat, and then got distracted with having to mop up a bloodied knee of a boy who'd fallen in the playground.

She was always busy at work, which was probably why she enjoyed it so much. There was no time for wallowing in her own problems when there were one hundred little people running around, all demanding her attention. The day went quickly, and before she knew it, she was picking Ollie up from afterschool club and walking him home. The boy chatted at a million miles an hour, and she tried to focus on everything he was saying, throwing in questions of her own when he broke to take a breath, but her mind kept going back to what Anna had told her about taking in foreign students.

She approached the house and spotted someone in the bushes beside the driveway.

"Lemmy. Come here, boy."

Her massive tabby cat emerged from the foliage, stretching lazily and yawning, as though he was more than happy to do things in his own time and keep her waiting. Finally, he sauntered over, and she bent and scooped him up in her arms. His fur was warm and dusty from dirt where he'd been rolling around. He was heavy, but she told herself he was just chunky.

"Haven't quite worked your way around to your summer body, have you, buddy?" she told the cat, burying her nose into his soft fur. "I know the feeling."

She carried him back into the house and emptied a sachet of supermarket brand food into his bowl. He tucked in, not caring that she wasn't able to afford any of the expensive stuff. She'd got Lemmy before Ollie was even conceived. He'd been a tiny, fluffy kitten, and she'd named him after the frontman of a rock band she'd loved in her what would now be considered emo years. The name didn't suit him in the slightest then, but somehow, she'd known he would grow into it, which he most definitely had. Ollie loved Lemmy too, and the cat often found his way into the boy's bed. She'd discover Lemmy lying alongside Ollie, purring with Ollie's arm slung around his waist, both their heads on the pillow.

So, no, she couldn't give up the cat, even though the money she spent on his food would have helped her have better meals for herself. She'd have gone hungry rather than be without him.

That evening she made dinner for Ollie—instant noodles topped with beans and a scraping of cheese—and then let him have a little unprecedented weekday television to allow her to go online and search what Anna had told her about boarding students. It seemed her colleague was right, and Kristen's heart sped up in both anticipation of all that extra money and the possibility of having someone in her home again. It had been just her and Ollie for so long now. She wasn't sure how it would be with another person in the house. At least if it was a student, she would still be the one in control, plus the university would screen the candidate before she put them up in her home. They would have to do things her way, as they'd be fully aware that she was putting them up, and this wasn't an equal share situation. This was still her house, and whoever stayed here would have to go by her rules.

She sucked in a breath. Besides, this wasn't about her. Sure, she might feel a bit awkward at first, but it could completely change things for Ollie. It often felt lonely here, just the two of them, and she was sure he'd love to have another younger person around. And it would mean he'd no longer find his mother crying in the hallway over a letter she'd just received, and he could go swimming with his friends, and out for lunch, and she could take him for days out at the zoo.

Her mind made up, Kristen pulled up the form she needed to fill in to apply to be a host and quickly filled it in and hit send. For all she knew, they might not need any more host families, but at least she'd done something proactive to try to change her situation.

Chapter Two

Kristen's phone had been ringing all afternoon, but she wasn't going to answer it. Not yet, anyway.

The number displayed belonged to her younger sister, Violet, and she knew answering the call was going to throw some kind of drama at her front door. Besides, she was at work, and they weren't supposed to deal with personal stuff outside of their lunch and coffee breaks, unless they were a real emergency. She was sure whatever Violet wanted would constitute an emergency in her mind, but not to Kristen. Yet she couldn't bring herself to switch the phone off, just in case.

She turned back to her computer, planning on focusing on work. There were several invoices that needed to be paid to the school's maintenance firm, and health and safety forms needed to be filled in for a visit from an outside puppet company that were coming in to perform to the reception class.

Her phone buzzed again, and she sighed and quickly leaned into her bag beside her chair to check the screen. She was sure it would be a text from Violet demanding to know why she hadn't picked up yet, but instead the little icon at the top of the screen informed her she had a new email in her personal account.

Her stomach lurched, and she sucked in a breath. Glancing up to make sure no one was watching, she opened her inbox. The email was from the housing people at the university.

Fluttery with adrenaline, she opened it.

Thank you for your enquiry. We do currently have openings for new host families. A home check would need to be completed to make sure the property is suitable. Please check the details of what's expected. Let us know when you're available.

She quickly wrote back. *Any day after four p.m. would be fine, and I'm home all weekend.* The sooner she could make this happen, the sooner she could stop worrying about money all the time.

Just as she hit send, the phone buzzed again, and Violet's name appeared on the screen.

"Shit."

Anna looked up from where she was sitting behind her desk on the other side of the room. "Problems?"

"Oh, just my sister. She's been calling me all afternoon."

"Shouldn't you call her back, then?"

She exhaled a long, troubled sigh. "Honestly, I'd rather not."

Anna pulled a face. "Problems again?"

"There always are with her."

Kristen hadn't told Anna the half of it. Violet seemed incapable of making a single sensible, adult decision. She was only two years younger than Kristen's thirty-one years but acted like she was ten years younger. While Kristen had been desperate to get married and have a family of her own, Violet avoided relationships. Or at least relationships that meant anything. Kristen wished she could try to have the upper hand on that side of things, but the minute she tried to bring up Violet's crazy way of picking up boyfriends for a matter of weeks, deciding they were definitely the one, even announcing she was engaged and getting married, only to break up with them again in a shower of dramatics and heartbreak, never got her anywhere. Violet would just say something along the lines of 'well, I'm hardly going to take relationship advice from someone who ended up divorced before she was even thirty' or 'you're hardly one to talk—where's your adoring man lately?' And then Kristen wouldn't have any way of getting back on the high horse.

The truth was that Violet was right in many ways. She couldn't give relationship advice. When she'd met Stephen, she'd been desperate to be in a committed relationship, and he'd seemed like the right guy for her, at first. He'd wined and dined her, they'd stayed up all night talking, and he'd told her all about how he couldn't wait to have kids and start a family. They'd been happy and in love, and because of that, she'd deliberately ignored his wandering eye and the appreciative glances he'd give to the waitresses when they were out, or the group of young women on the streets. She'd fallen pregnant within the first year of them being together—a case of the pill not working after she'd needed antibiotics for a dental infection—and of course he'd insisted they get married. She'd been delighted and had felt like her life was heading on the right track, but as the wedding got closer, and she only got bigger, her entire body swelling with the pregnancy, she knew the relationship wasn't quite right. The further into the pregnancy she got, the more she noticed that wandering eye, but she convinced herself it was understandable. She was massive, her stomach swollen and distended, her breasts covered in thick blue veins, and she suddenly had a double chin that had appeared from nowhere. On top of that, she suffered almost constantly with indigestion, and, frankly, the amount of wind she produced was humiliating, so she didn't blame him in the slightest for not being interested in having sex with her.

On her wedding day, she felt fat and hideous, and not in the slightest bit beautiful. Violet had shown up with some guy she was dating at the time, and the two of them drank whiskey from a hipflask, and the hotel where they'd had their small reception had threatened to throw the two of them out for bringing alcohol onto the premises. Stephen had spent most of the reception drinking and hanging out with his buddies, so on their wedding night, feeling exhausted and miserable, she went to bed alone. He'd stumbled in several hours later, managing to kick off his shoes, before collapsing into bed beside her, and he had been snoring within seconds.

Deep down, she'd known then that this wasn't going to work, but still she'd tried to convince herself it would be different after the baby arrived. Of course, it wasn't. While she adored Ollie more than anything in the world, the tension between her and Stephen only increased. She hated her new post-baby body, and Stephen didn't seem overly keen on it either. He started staying out later and later, and, one night, eventually didn't come home at all. He admitted that he'd met someone else, but convinced her it was over, and that he'd change. It had been hard, but she'd been terrified of having to do this alone. Things got better for a year or so, and then started to slide again. Eventually, he admitted this was never going to work, and that he was only there for Ollie, and he moved out. Within a few months, he met someone else—the same person he was married to now. The worst part in Kristen's mind was that she'd convinced herself it was because he couldn't handle the responsibilities of being a dad, and that was why he'd left, but the woman he'd met already had a child, and then she'd fallen pregnant with his baby, too. It hadn't been about the pregnancy or the child, it had simply been that he had never really loved her.

But at least she'd had Ollie out of the whole fiasco, and really, that was the only thing that mattered.

With a sigh, Kristen swiped green to answer. Quickly, she rose to her feet, and hurried out of the office, towards the staff toilets so she wouldn't be seen on her phone outside of break time.

"What's wrong, Violet?" she said, pressing the phone to her ear as she pushed into the toilet stall. "I'm at work."

She could barely hear what her sister was saying through the sniffs and sobs.

"Jesus, Violet. What's the matter? Take a breath and talk to me."

"I hate it!" Her sister's voice came down the line. "I just don't know how I'm going to be able to face the world every day!"

"What are you talking about?"

"I had my hair cut. It's really short. It looks awful."

Anger boiled up inside her. "You're kidding me, right? You've been calling me all afternoon, knowing I'm at work, because you don't like a haircut?"

"You don't understand. It makes me look like a bloke."

She could hear the slurring in Violet's words. "Have you been drinking?"

"Only a little. Just to take the edge off."

Kristen gave a growl of disgust and swiped the screen, ending the call. What the hell was the matter with her sister? Okay, they hadn't had the best of upbringings, but Kristen still felt she at least managed to claw her way through life. Why did every little thing send Violet into dramatics?

She left the bathroom, shaking her head, still caught up in the ridiculousness of her sister's life, only to collide straight into a broad, male body in a suit.

She looked up, her phone still clutched in her hand. "Oh, Andrew. Excuse me."

The headteacher caught sight of the phone. "I hope you weren't just on a personal call, Kristen? You know the rules about that."

"Sorry. It was an emergency. My sister... err... lost her house keys. She can't get in and I have a spare set."

"That isn't really your problem, is it? And it certainly isn't the school's problem. It shouldn't really be dealt with on school time."

"No, of course not." Her cheeks burned. She wanted to retaliate, but instead she shut her mouth and swallowed her words. She needed this job far more than they needed her.

He ducked his head in a nod. "I expect to see you back at your desk then."

She forced a smile. "Right away."

Why did Violet always manage to get her in trouble? Things hadn't been any different when they'd been younger either and trying to deal with their mother. They hadn't thought she was any different to other mothers until they'd hit their preteens, and the shutters had been brought down. It seemed the sight of Kristen's budding breasts had thrown their mother's already protective nature into overdrive, and she'd desperately wanted to prevent the two girls from growing up.

Kristen had done everything she could to try to shelter Violet from their mother's behaviour, but she hadn't realised she'd still be taking care of her little sister when they were both grown.

Just for once, she wished she had someone she could turn to, instead of everyone always relying on her.

Chapter Three

Kristen gritted her teeth and strained against the big wooden desk. It was far heavier than it looked, and for once, she wished she still had Stephen around.

"Mummy," came a little voice from the doorway. "What are you doing?"

She lifted the desk again and it shifted a few inches. "Moving your desk into the spare room." She panted with the effort.

His lower lip pouted. "But that's *my* desk."

Dropping the item of furniture, she turned back to him. "I know, sweetie, but remember how we talked about having someone come and stay here for a little while, to help me out with some stuff?" Ollie nodded, and she continued. "Well, there are certain things they'll need to have in their room, and a desk is one of them. They'll be studying, so it's really important they have one."

He wasn't convinced. "But I go to school, too. I'm learning. I need a desk."

She crouched to bring herself down to his level and took his hand. "Hey, how about, once our new student moves in, I buy you a whole new desk?"

It pained her to say it, knowing that first week's money could go on far more important things. Ollie was only five, after all. It wasn't as though he really needed one. He could just as easily sit at the dining room table, or even on the floor, but the woman from the university housing was due over in less than an hour, and she needed to get this done. Not only that, she didn't want Ollie having a meltdown while the woman was here. She needed him to be happy and enthusiastic, and not sulking or crying because he thought he was going to lose his stuff to a stranger staying in his home.

His eyes brightened at the suggestion. "A new one?"

She thought of the money she'd save if she managed to pick on up from the charity shop. "Well, new to us anyway."

Ollie pursed his lips, his nose wrinkling as he considered her offer, and then his face relaxed in a smile. "Okay, then. I think I'd like that."

The knot of tension inside her relaxed a fraction. "Good boy. Now go and play for a bit while Mummy finishes doing this."

He turned and thundered back down the stairs, giving a roar at some imaginary creature he was fighting as he jumped down the bottom two.

"And don't jump down the stairs," she shouted after him, even though she knew he wouldn't pay the slightest bit of attention.

Kristen turned back to the desk. It was surprisingly heavy, but she needed to get it moved, even if it meant putting her back out doing it. Time was whizzing by, and she didn't want to be unprepared for the inspection.

Heaving, and shoving, and swearing under her breath so Ollie didn't hear her, she gradually edged her way out of the room with the desk and dragged it across the hallway into the spare room. The room was only large enough for a single bed, but there was enough space for the desk and a small chest of drawers, and it had a built-in wardrobe for the student's clothes. She wished they had a second bathroom in the house—it would be weird sharing a bathroom with a stranger—but they would have to make do. A private bathroom wasn't a prerequisite of being a host family, so that was good enough for her.

She straightened and pushed her hair from her face, the light brown strands clinging to her sweaty forehead. She took one final look around the room. It wasn't perfect, but it wasn't bad either. In an ideal world, she'd have liked to have bought new bedding, but there was no way she could afford to do that right now. And anyway, in an ideal world, she wouldn't be needing to bring a stranger into her home to help pay the gas bill, so there was that.

The doorbell jingled through the house.

"She's here, Mummy!" Ollie yelled from downstairs.

By the time she joined him, he was already hopping up and down at the front door in excitement. They didn't get many visitors.

Kristen took a breath, plastered on a smile, and opened the door.

A woman in her fifties with a brightly coloured scarf, long beads draped around her neck, and knee-high boots stood on her doorstep. Kind blue eyes were framed with a pair of turquoise glasses.

"You must be Mrs. Scott," she said. "I'm Nancy McFadden from the University Housing."

Kristen stepped back, pulling Ollie against the front of her legs to keep him out of the way. "Yes, hello. We're expecting you. Please, come in."

"Thank you." The woman stepped into the house with them, casting her gaze around. Kristen tried not to feel as though both she and her home were being judged, even though that was the exact reason for Nancy McFadden's visit.

Ollie stayed close, pressing himself up against his mother's legs, even though he'd been so excited about having a visitor before she'd arrived.

Nancy smiled down at Ollie. "Are you excited about having a student come and stay?"

Ollie shrugged shyly and clung to Kristen's leg. "I guess so."

Nancy smiled at his response.

"Why don't you go and play with your Lego in the other room?" Kristen encouraged him. "Let the grownups talk."

"We'll be talking about some really boring stuff," Nancy said.

Ollie nodded and unravelled his arms from Kristen's legs to vanish into the kitchen.

Nancy turned her attention to Kristen. "So, Mrs. Scott—"

"Oh, it's Kristen, please," she corrected her. "And I'm not married. I mean, I was, once. But not anymore." Her face burned at her admission. Why was it every time she acknowledged her divorce it was like admitting a failure, and she was instantly expecting to be judged.

But Nancy leaned in and lowered her voice, so Ollie didn't hear. "Oh, neither am I. Think we're best rid of them, personally."

She surprised a laugh out of Kristen. "I couldn't agree more."

"Good. So, let's move on." Nancy glanced down at the paperwork. "I understand you're after a mature student rather than one of our younger ones."

"Yes, that's right. I think I'd feel more comfortable with an adult. I don't have much experience of teenagers, apart from when I was one myself, and with Ollie in the house, I'm not sure I could take on that kind of responsibility."

"Of course. I completely understand. Well, your location is great for the university. I noticed a bus stop just down the road, and the buses seem to run regularly."

"Yes, they do," Kristen agreed. "Oh, and I have a cat. Is that okay? I did put it down on the application form."

"That's fine. We'll make sure you're not matched with someone who has allergies or is scared of them, that's all."

She exhaled a sigh of relief. She already felt guilty having Lemmy. When she was struggling to put food on the table, that couple of quid a week in cat food made a difference. She didn't have pet insurance, simply because she couldn't afford the extra ten pounds a month, and lived in fear of something happening to him where she'd end up with a massive bill she wouldn't be able to pay. She'd wondered if it would be better to give him over to someone else, but just the thought broke her heart, and she knew Ollie would be devastated, too. Their little family had already been torn apart, and losing Lemmy as well felt like one step too far. People said, 'he's only a cat', but to her, he was another little person, just one that happened to have four paws and whiskers. She'd have no more given him up than she would Ollie, but if she hadn't been able to become a host family because of him, it would have just been another thing to feel guilty about.

"Right, then," Nancy said, "I'll just take a look at the room."

"Of course."

Kristen led her up the stairs to the bedroom. Ollie had noticed the movement and abandoned his Lego in the other room to scamper up after them. Kristen prayed he wasn't going to say anything about the desk. She didn't want it to look like she was depriving her son to get the student.

Nancy stepped in and looked around. "This all looks great. Can I see the rest of the house?"

"Of course."

Kristen showed her the bathroom, and then back downstairs to the kitchen.

Nancy looked around and then turned back to her. "I can't see any reason we can't accept you as a host family. We will need to run DBS checks, though I'm assuming you don't have some secret criminal past we should be aware of?"

Kristen laughed nervously and thought back to her mother. "No, not at all."

"Good. Well, we'll be in touch."

"Thanks so much."

Kristen showed Nancy out, and then closed the door behind her and let out a shaky sigh. She thought that had gone well, but she wasn't someone who counted her chickens.

She just hoped she'd done enough.

Chapter Four

The week passed by as normal, and she didn't hear anything from the student housing people. She tried not to think about it, knowing that obsessing whether she'd been accepted wouldn't make any difference to the result.

This weekend was Stephen's turn to have Ollie, but it was getting late. Stephen should have been here over an hour ago, but there was still no sign of him.

These weekends should be times she'd be looking forward to a chance to have a break, to take a long bath, or have a lie in, or just read a good book, but instead she found herself dreading them. Ollie's behaviour tended to get worse when he was building up to a weekend with his dad. She understood why. He built himself up into such a nervous, over-excited state that he wasn't able to control himself. He tore around the house at a million miles an hour, shouting at invisible monsters he was fighting, and throwing his toys down the stairs, despite Kristen telling him to stop it. Dealing with him like this was exhausting, and by the time they'd been back from school for an hour, she could already tell she was short-tempered and snappish. She didn't like herself when she was in this kind of mood, and Ollie seemed to know how to press all her buttons. They were normally so close, but it was like the prospect of missing each other made them push each other away instead of enjoying the last couple of hours together. Perhaps it was a self-preservation thing.

Kristen paced anxiously, peering out of the window for any sign of her ex-husband's car. Ollie was getting tired now, his chin dropping onto his narrow chest as he watched Paw Patrol on television. She didn't normally like him watching television in the evenings, but she'd been getting desperate.

She picked up the phone and dialled Stephen's number for the fifth time that evening. It went straight through to answer phone.

"Where the hell are you?" she hissed, trying to keep her voice down so Ollie didn't hear. "You need to call me right away!"

The agreement was that he came to pick Ollie up as soon as he finished work at five-thirty. Ollie went to bed by seven, so much later and it wouldn't be worth him going. She had a sinking in her stomach that this was just going to be a repeat of the previous weekend Stephen had been supposed to have him. It wasn't that she didn't want Ollie at home—he was her entire life and she loved having him with her—but she hated to see her son's disappointment, and she hated being the one who had to make up lies about how much his father was missing him and how he couldn't help it. The truth burned like acid inside her, eating her up, but she knew telling her son would only be making herself feel better and hurting him, and she'd never do that.

The phone buzzed, and she snatched it up. "Where the hell are you?"

"I'm sorry. Something came up at work. I'm still here. It's going to be a late one."

She was sure she could hear the low chatter of a busy place in the background, more akin to a bar than an office. "Yeah, right."

"Don't be like that, Kristen. I'll pick him up first thing in the morning, right after Lyla has done her swimming lesson."

Lyla was the new wife's six-year-old daughter from a previous relationship.

"So that won't be first thing, will it?" she snapped. "You're putting taking Lyla ahead of Ollie again."

"I have to. I promised I'd take her."

Her voice lifted in anger. "You promised you'd be here to take Ollie for the weekend. Lyla gets you every day, but Ollie never gets to see you. How do you think that's fair?"

"This isn't about what's fair."

"No, apparently not, because Lyla isn't even your flesh and blood, and yet you treat her more like your child than you do Ollie!"

She felt horrible bringing up his relationship to Lyla, like some bitter and twisted witch—the epitome of an evil ex-wife. The little girl was lucky to have a father figure in her life. It was something Kristen had never had herself, and she remembered wishing so badly for her mysterious father to just show up at the door one day and whisk her and Violet away from the madness that was her mother. Of course, that never happened, and now she was begrudging a little girl of the same dream she'd had as a child.

"Lyla might not be my flesh and blood, but she's still my daughter. I've been raising her since she was three." He exhaled a long, frustrated sigh and then continued. "Families are complicated. Sometimes you have to be a little bit flexible, Kristen."

She was steaming with anger. "Flexible? I'm always flexible. I have to be, but only to accommodate you!"

The kitchen door opened, and big, sad eyes blinked back at her. "He's not coming, is he?"

Kristen pressed her lips together, trying to hold back her emotion. "Your son wants to speak to you. I suggest you explain to him what's happened this time." She pressed the phone to Ollie's ear.

"Hi, Daddy."

Kristen struggled with tears of frustration and anger and disappointment, but she gave Ollie a smile of encouragement. She knew what it was like to grow up without a father in her life, and she didn't want him to have to do the same. So even though it half killed her, she did her best to smooth things over.

Her heart broke as she overheard his side of the conversation. "That's okay. I understand... I know you're really busy.... Yes, okay. See you tomorrow."

If Stephen didn't turn up in the morning, she knew she'd struggle to hold herself back. She felt as though she was constantly wearing a mask to deal with her ex-husband, knowing remaining as civil as possible was only good for Ollie. It was so fucking hard, though, and there were times where she genuinely found herself close to physical violence. Lisa, the new wife, probably thought she was a complete psycho, and though Stephen kept the two of them apart, she daydreamed conversations where she'd tell Lisa that the only reason she might act crazy at times was because Stephen had made her that way.

Except that wasn't completely true, was it? There had always been a little craziness in her family, and though she tended to think Violet had gotten more of her mother's genes than she had, who knew what she was capable of deep down?

THE FOLLOWING MORNING, Stephen turned up on time, and Kristen was able to kiss her son goodbye and finally take a breath. She missed Ollie horribly when he wasn't there, but she'd been terrified Stephen was going to let him down once again, and then she'd have yet another fight on her hands.

She'd slept badly the previous night, too stressed out from her fight with Stephen to relax and worrying about how things would play out that morning. She'd promised herself she'd go back to bed if and when Stephen did show up, but now Ollie was gone, and curling up back in bed, all on her own, felt depressing. Instead, she made herself a cup of tea and thought she might go for a walk down by the river instead, get some endorphins going. If she was still tired after that, perhaps she would take a little nap on the sofa.

Her phone rang, and she checked the screen to see a number she didn't recognise. For a moment, she considered not answering it, but then decided it would bug her all day if she didn't answer.

"Hello?"

"Is that Kristen Scott?"

"Yes, speaking?"

"Hi, my name's Jess York and I'm calling from the university housing."

She immediately perked up. "Oh, yes, hello. What can I do for you?"

"We've had a last-minute change of circumstances with one of our other host families and need a replacement. It's all a bit last minute, I'm afraid, but the students are already on their way here, and one of them doesn't have anywhere to stay."

"Already on their way here? When do they arrive?"

"This afternoon, by coach. I'd need you to pick him up at three p.m., if at all possible?"

"Oh, right. Umm…" Her mind was racing. She'd need to get extra food in, as providing meals was part of the agreement. Did she have time to get everything ready? It would mean an extra two hundred pounds going into the pot for next week. "That would be fine. Three o'clock, you said?"

"That's right. At the bus station in town."

"Great. I'll be there."

She hung up and suddenly realised she hadn't asked a single question about the person who would be staying in her home.

Kristen spent the next few hours in a whirlwind of panic, worried she was making a huge mistake by letting a complete stranger into her home. She told herself the person would barely be past childhood, and they'd be more interested in their studies than anything else, but still she worried. She tidied up the room again and made sure everything was in place. She provided clean towels, and then worried if she should have provided toiletries as well, or if they'd bring them with them, then she went down to the shops and picked up another loaf of bread, some pasta, and potatoes to do jacket spuds with. Teenage boys ate a lot, she knew that much, so whatever was cheap and in bulk was what she'd be feeding him. Next week, when the first week's payment came through, she'd be able to afford to be a little more luxurious with the meals, but for this week they'd simply have to make do. She hoped he wasn't going to say anything about the food. She'd be embarrassed if he felt it wasn't good enough, but then youngsters preferred simple things, didn't they? She knew when she tried to feed Ollie anything out of the ordinary, he always turned his nose up.

Finally, the time rolled around for her to leave. She felt wired and anxious about picking up the student, but she tried to quash the emotions. This was a perfectly normal thing to do. Plenty of families took in foreign students. She almost wished Ollie was with her. At least he'd be able to act as a bit of a buffer and a distraction. But no, she was being a big baby. She couldn't rely on a five-year-old to ward off her anxiety.

Kristen got in the car and drove the twenty minutes into the middle of town to the bus station. She had arrived early, but that was better than being late, even if it meant she now had even more time to worry. She hoped Ollie wasn't going to be shocked when he came home to find someone else living in their house. They'd talked about it happening, but talking was very different from the reality of waking up every day to have someone else sitting across from you at the kitchen table.

A small group of people were already waiting. One of them was wearing a t-shirt with the university emblem on the front and held a clipboard. Kristen had been hoping to see Nancy McFadden again, but she guessed the woman was allowed a day off.

Kristen smiled nervously as she approached.

"Umm, hi." She waited until she was noticed, which she was, and the woman holding the clipboard smiled in return.

"I'm Kristen Scott. I'm filling in as a last-minute host family. I'm sorry, I forgot to ask who I was going to be picking up."

"Ah, yes." The woman scanned the clipboard and stabbed her pen down on a line. "You're picking up a Swedish student, Haiden Lindgren. He's here studying for a semester for his master's degree in Business."

"Master's degree?" She tried not to sound surprised and failed. Wasn't that what they did after they'd already completed a full degree? That would make whoever she was picking up in at least their early twenties.

"Yes, that's right." She frowned down at the clipboard. "You did want a mature student, didn't you?"

"Yes, yes. Absolutely. I guess I thought they'd all be in their late teens."

"Oh, most of them are."

"Right."

Her nerves increased. She had the sudden feeling that everything was out of her control and she'd been plunged into a situation that she'd had no choice in. Of course, that was rubbish. She'd actively tried to get to this point. She needed to focus on the money and the benefit that was going to bring to their lives, and not the small amount of discomfort she'd experience having some strange man living in her house. Besides, she needed to make Ollie comfortable with this, and she wouldn't be able to do that if she was freaking out.

Taking a deep breath, she looked around at everyone else waiting. Some of them seemed to know each other and stood around chatting, while others appeared bored, staring at their phones.

"Ah, here they come," the woman with the clipboard announced.

A large, expensive looking coach pulled into the bus station. Kristen's heart pattered, her mouth running dry with nerves. She pulled anxiously on the strap of her handbag and opened and closed her fists.

The coach pulled in beside them, and something beneath the vehicle hissed as it lowered to the ground. The doors opened, and another adult with a clipboard stood just inside the door, checking off students as they filed off the coach. Kristen scanned each boy as they piled off, wondering which one would be coming home with her.

Long legs appeared from the steps of the coach, followed by a lean torso and broad shoulders. She could already tell he was a lot older than the other students. Stupidly, her heart beat faster, and heat flooded to her face. She'd been expecting some spotty teenager, not a grown man.

The person with the clipboard looked over, craning his neck, and the woman she'd spoken to when she'd first arrived pointed her out.

Jesus, how tall was he? She guessed at least six feet two, and he dwarfed her five feet five frame. He was definitely young, that was for sure, but he also wasn't a teenager. She guessed early to mid-twenties. Considering she was going to be living with this tall blond stranger, she figured she'd learn plenty about him over the next few weeks and months.

Awkwardly, she lifted a hand in a wave and gave a half smile.

The man, Haiden Lindgren, caught her eye, and the woman with the clipboard nodded. He grabbed a case from underneath the coach then headed over to her.

"Hello." He offered her a wide smile filled with white teeth. "I believe you're to be my host for the next three months."

"That's right." She stuck out her hand, wondering if the Swedes greeted people like the Spanish and French, and he was expecting a kiss instead. She hoped not. She didn't want to get that close to him. He seemed happy with the handshake and placed his large palm around hers.

"Kristen Scott," she said. "Please, just call me Kristen."

"It's very good to meet you, Kristen. I'm Haiden."

"It's good to meet you, too. I hope you'll be comfortable in my home. This is the first time I've taken in a foreign student."

"Did you and your husband decide to make use of an empty room?"

"Oh, there's no husband, but I do have a son. He's called Ollie, and he's five. I have a cat, too, called Lemmy. I'll make sure I keep them both out of your way." She was babbling, and the realisation made her shrink inside.

"No need at all," he replied. "I've always liked cats, and I used to be a boy, so I don't mind them either."

She gave a small laugh. "Of course. Well, my car is just over here." She checked behind him. "Are there any more bags? I can help carry one."

"Nope, this is it." Just the case and a backpack slung over his shoulder.

His English was already almost perfect. If it wasn't for the slight accent—the sharper 't's' and the more clipped words—she might not have even guessed he wasn't from here.

He did have that typical Nordic look, though, with the blond hair, blue eyes, and tanned skin. He radiated youth and good health, and Kristen felt even older, chubbier, and paler than usual.

She led him towards where she'd parked the car. It was an old model, but it had always been reliable in the five years since she'd bought it, just after Ollie was born. It was a good thing, too. She wouldn't have been able to afford a vehicle that kept breaking down on her. But other than its MOTs and a couple of minor problems, the car had been a good workhorse.

She opened the boot for Haiden to throw his case inside, and then went to the driver's side while he went to the passenger door.

"Do you drive?" she asked him.

"Yes, I do back home, but it's not worth me hiring a car while I'm here. I'm told you have a good public transport system which will allow me to get around."

"Yes, that's right. The bus is pretty regular. The housing people checked all of that before they approved me as a host."

"That's good."

She started the car and pulled it out of the bus station and into traffic. It felt strange driving around with this handsome young man in the passenger seat. She'd been a single mother for several years now—there hadn't been anyone since Stephen left—but that didn't mean she couldn't appreciate the company of a handsome male. She was only just thirty-one; it wasn't as though she had one foot in the grave.

"How far from here do you live?" he asked.

She glanced over to him as she drove. "Not too far. About twenty minutes in the traffic, but it's really only a couple of miles out of town. The bus will get you there quicker since they can use the bus lanes."

"You know," he said, watching her, "you're not exactly what I expected."

She felt the intensity of his gaze and was relieved to be able to concentrate on the road, so she didn't have to meet his blue eyes. "You're not exactly what I was expecting either."

"No? What were you expecting?"

"Umm... someone younger, I guess."

He chuckled. "And I was expecting someone older. Someone more... motherly."

"I'm motherly!" she exclaimed in surprise.

"Not as far as I can see."

Heat rose in a flush up her chest and into her cheeks. She wished Ollie was here so she could wave the boy under this attractive man's nose like a defence mechanism. But she shook the thought out of her head. She was being ridiculous. This gorgeous twenty-something was not interested in someone like her. She was probably ten years his senior and was still carrying baby-weight, despite Ollie being five years old now. He'd be used to tall blonde Swedish girls, not short, slightly dumpy brunette English women—and a mother, at that. She was projecting, that was all. Just because she'd been instantly hit by her attraction to him didn't mean it was the slightest bit reciprocated. He was being polite and nice to her because he was staying in her home for the next twelve weeks. She had to pull herself together or she'd end up making a fool out of herself.

Thankfully, the traffic wasn't bad, and the drive back home only took fifteen minutes. She pulled up on the road outside of her house, happy to get a spot close to the front door.

"Here we are," she announced. "Home sweet home."

He craned his head to look out of the window. "It looks very nice."

"Thanks."

The house wasn't anything flash, but it was a reasonable size three bedroom in a good area. The back garden was big enough for Ollie to play in, and they didn't have any busy roads nearby, the location quiet. She wondered what sort of background Haiden came from. The only thing she knew about Sweden was Ikea, and she didn't think he'd appreciate her mentioning the big, multinational store. She bet it was what everyone talked about when they found out where he was from—flatpack furniture and meatballs.

"This way."

Haiden claimed his case from the boot, and she led him towards the house and opened the front door. She'd made an effort to clean the place before she'd left to pick him up, so the waft of polish and bleach met her nose. They both stepped into the house, and Haiden put down his luggage, the big case taking up too much space in the small entrance hall.

"I'll show you your room," she said, already heading for the stairs.

He followed her up, and she led him into the spare room that would be his for the next twelve weeks. "Here you go."

Haiden stepped in and looked around.

The shoddiness of the bedroom embarrassed her. "I'm sorry it's not more... upmarket."

He threw his bag on the bed and turned to her. "It's great, thanks. It's got everything I need."

"So, have you got any student... activities... arranged for the weekend?"

"No, they tend to just let us settle in, and then we get started first thing Monday morning."

He seemed too big for the room, as though he would need to bend his neck in order to fit in. She wished for a moment that she'd given him Ollie's room, and had Ollie in here, but she could never have done that to her son. She didn't want Ollie to feel like he was being turfed out of his own bedroom for some blond stranger. Very blond. Very blue-eyed. Yet with tanned skin. It was a typical look of people from his country, but here he seemed exotic and out of place.

"Oh, right."

She wished he'd had something already in the diary. Now it meant he'd be here in the house.

God, she was going to have to spend Saturday night eating a meal with a strange man, just the two of them. She hadn't done that since before Stephen had left.

"I'll let you get settled," she said, turning from the room and hoping he'd give her a little space to get settled herself. "Hope you like pasta. It's what I'm making for dinner tonight."

"As long as it's not served with Ikea meatballs, I love it."

The teasing was clear in his tone, and to her surprise, she found herself smiling as she headed downstairs.

Chapter Five

Kristen stared down at the two plates of pesto pasta and the sides of garlic bread, and wished she'd thought to buy something with meat in it. It had been a long time since she'd cooked for a male over the age of five, and right now the meal she was providing looked far too vegetarian. She hoped Haiden wasn't going to be disappointed.

She went to the fridge to take out the parmesan cheese and paused to stare wistfully at a bottle of dry white wine that was in there. It had been a present from Anna for her birthday the previous month, and she still hadn't opened it. She never bought alcohol herself—not when the money could go on Ollie—and she'd practically forgotten it was in there. But now it was Saturday night, and she was having dinner with an actual adult, and she suddenly wondered if it would be inappropriate to offer a glass of wine with dinner. It wasn't as though he was underage.

No, she shook the thought from her head. That wouldn't be right at all. Maybe he was old enough to drink, but she shouldn't be the one providing the alcohol.

Footsteps landed heavy on the stairs, and she grabbed the block of parmesan and slammed the fridge door shut. She straightened and brushed her hair away from her face, hoping she didn't look too hot and sweaty after standing over the oven.

"Something smells good," Haiden said as he walked into the kitchen.

She threw him a smile. "I hope it's okay. It's only something simple."

"Anything I can do to help?"

"Nope, just take a seat, and I'll bring it over."

He slid into a chair and placed his forearms on the table as he waited. They were tanned, attractive forearms, ridged with defined muscle. He wore a casual shirt that seemed too mature for a student, but was rolled up at the sleeves, as though he was deliberately trying to show off his best feature. Not that the rest of him wasn't attractive, too. She didn't think she'd ever been hit with such a visceral attraction to someone in her whole life, and all the alarm bells inside her were jangling. It wasn't as though she could go back to university housing and ask for someone different on the grounds that her current houseguest was too damned good looking.

She finished serving up the spaghetti and slid the two plates onto the table, then added a bowl of salad and some garlic bread.

"This all looks great," he said, picking up his fork.

"It's nothing, really." She was unusually flustered. "Oh, I forgot the parmesan." She hopped back up again and ran back to grab the block of cheese and the grater. Again, the chilled bottle of white wine called to her, but she ignored it.

"So, tell me about your family back home?" she asked as she added a sprinkle of cheese to the top of her pasta and then offered Haiden some.

He shrugged. "There isn't much to tell. My mother and father are still together, and I have a younger sister called Linda."

"Are you all close?"

"Yes, very." He looked down at his plate and twiddled spaghetti around on his fork. "I'm still living with them while I'm studying."

"Oh, you live with your parents?"

Somehow, that had surprised her. She couldn't imagine this big, grown man still living at home.

He must have picked up on her thoughts. "It's only because I'm moving around while I'm studying. There's no point in me paying rent on an apartment while I'm in a different country."

Her cheeks heated. "No, of course not. That wouldn't make sense at all."

They both fell silent as they tucked into their food.

"Feel free to use the house phone if you need to call them," she offered, needing to break the silence. She instantly regretted the suggestion. What if he took her up on the offer and spent hours on the phone? She could never afford to pay for expensive, long distance phone calls.

"That's kind of you, but I have my mobile phone, so I'll just call them from that."

Of course, he had a phone. It was stupid of her to not think of it.

"Perhaps we should swap numbers," he said with a lopsided smile. "You know, just in case we need to get in touch for any reason."

He was asking for her phone number.

"Sure, that makes sense. I need to get you a key cut, too. I should have done it earlier, but I wasn't expecting to take in a student so soon. I'll be around most of the time though, and I only work up the road, at the local school, should you find yourself unable to get in when you need to."

"Is it the same school where your son goes?"

She smiled at the mention of Ollie. "Yes, that's right. He loves it there."

Haiden nodded. "That's good. I'll know where to find you if I need you, then."

"Yes," she said. "Come and find me, whatever you need."

"SINCE YOU HUNG UP ON me last time," Violet announced, her hands on her hips, "and didn't even bother to phone me back, I had to assume that you obviously don't give a damn about whether I'm alive or dead."

It was Sunday morning, and Kristen had opened the door, thinking Stephen had brought Ollie home early, only to find her sister standing on the doorstep.

Kristen rolled her eyes. "Don't be ridiculous, Violet. I've been busy, that's all, and I figured a bad haircut was hardly a life or death matter." She stared at her sister, eyeing up the infamous haircut. "What did you even have done? It looks exactly the same."

"Ugh! How can you say that?" She flicked out her brunette locks, a shade darker than Kristen's hair. "I only asked for a trim and she took loads off."

"It doesn't look any different to me."

"That's because I hardly see you anymore. It had grown, and then the hairdresser chopped it all off. I won't be going back there again." She glanced over Kristen's shoulder. "Anyway, aren't you going to let me in for a cup of tea? Where's that handsome nephew of mine?"

Kristen sighed and stepped to one side to allow Violet inside. "Ollie's with his dad this weekend."

"The asshole actually showed up, then?"

"Yeah, but not until the Saturday. He bailed on him on Friday night."

"God, Stephen is such a—"

Violet had been heading into the kitchen, but she cut off abruptly and turned back to Kristen. She lowered her voice to a whisper. "There's a man sitting at your kitchen table."

"Oh, yeah. He's staying for a while."

Her eyes widened. "You got yourself a man? A hot man!"

Kristen's face flared with heat. Violet hadn't bothered keeping her voice down for that last sentence.

"No!" she hissed back. "It's nothing like that. He's from Sweden, and he's studying at the university. I'm renting the spare room out to him, that's all."

Her expression faded a little, but then brightened again. "Does that mean he's single?"

Kristen's stomach lurched. "Uh-uh. No way. Don't even think about it, Violet. He is seriously off the table. I mean it. I need the income this is bringing in, and if you pull one of your usual relationship disasters, you're going to make things really difficult for me."

Her mouth dropped open. "What do you mean, my usual relationship disasters? Not all my relationships end badly. You never know, he might be the one." She waggled her eyebrows.

"No. I mean it. Besides, he's far too young for you."

"Rubbish. I'm still in my twenties."

Kristen scoffed a laugh. "Barely."

Looking at Violet was like getting a real-life idea of how she'd have looked herself had she never got married and had Ollie. She didn't want to feel jealous, since she had Ollie, and would never change that for all the world, but she did envy Violet's high, perky boobs, and her impossibly flat stomach. Her sister probably had never even worried about cellulite, or grey hairs, or stretch marks. Violet was effortlessly comfortable in her own skin, confident in knowing she was young and beautiful, and men found her attractive. Kristen had felt that way about herself many years ago, but pregnancy and motherhood had changed all of that, and she could barely imagine how horrified she'd be to take her clothes off in front of a man she liked. She couldn't see how any guy would possibly find what she saw in the mirror to be attractive. Deep down, she understood how Stephen's betrayal and his clear dislike of her pregnant and post-baby body had wrecked her self-esteem, and she probably wasn't as bad as she felt she was, but even so, she couldn't imagine letting another man see her naked.

"Well, if he's going to be living here, you still need to introduce me," Violet insisted.

Kristen sighed. Her sister was probably right. Haiden must already think they were acting strangely by standing out in the hallway whispering to one another like a couple of schoolgirls.

"Okay, fine. But behave yourself."

Violet fluttered her eyelashes. "Don't I always?"

Kristen wasn't even going to answer that. Violet had already turned and flounced into the kitchen, and Kristen followed.

"Hi!" Violet chirped. "I'm Violet, Kristen's sister. You must be the new lodger."

Kristen watched Haiden's gaze flick over Violet's shoulder towards her, and she gave him a tight apologetic smile in return.

"Yes, I'm Haiden. It's nice to meet you." He half stood and shook Violet's hand.

Kristen inwardly cringed as Violet held his hand a moment too long, and Haiden practically had to tug his fingers out of her grip.

"I'll leave you to your catch up," he told them, rising to stand fully. "I'll be up in my room, preparing for my first classes tomorrow."

"What are you studying?" Violet asked, twiddling a tendril of hair around her finger.

"A master's degree in business."

"Looks and brains," she said approvingly.

Kristen didn't miss how he blushed beneath his tan. He gathered up the paper he was reading and moved past them to leave the room. The two women waited until his footsteps had reached the top of the stairs before they spoke again.

Violet pulled a face at Kristen. "Too much?"

She rolled her eyes. "Just a bit."

"And he's going to be here for the next twelve weeks?"

"Yeah, so please be good. I know it's asking a lot from you, but I really can't afford to mess this up."

Violet lifted three fingers in a Girl Guide salute. "You have my word."

Chapter Six

Shortly after she managed to ferry Violet out of the house, Stephen turned up with Ollie.

"Hey, sweetie," she said, pulling her son against her body and giving him a squeeze. She placed a kiss to the top of his head, inhaling the sweet scent of his soft hair. "You have fun at your dad's?"

"Yeah, it was okay," Ollie said in a monotone voice and without a smile.

She exchanged an awkward glance with Stephen.

Her ex-husband shrugged. "He wouldn't go to sleep last night. Kept getting up and was asking for you."

Her heart tugged at the idea of her boy not being able to sleep without her. "You could have FaceTimed me or something. I'd have been able to say goodnight to him, then. He might have slept better."

"I can't get into that kind of routine, calling you whenever he needs something. It's not a good habit to get into."

She knew he was right. Stephen was still Ollie's dad, and he needed to be able to deal with things on his own, but that didn't make her feel any better. She hated not being able to be there when Ollie needed her.

"Hey, there's someone inside who I want you to meet," she said to Ollie, wanting to tell him about Haiden before he went inside and found a strange man sitting in their living room.

"You remember how I said about us taking in foreign students, and we got the room ready and everything?"

Ollie stared up at her with wide eyes and nodded.

"Well," she continued, "they needed someone to fill in this weekend, and so we have someone staying with us for a while. His name is Haiden and I think you'll really like him. He's from Sweden."

Stephen was staring at her the entire time, and when she finished, he cleared his throat. "Umm, don't you think I should have been consulted about this?"

She turned to him with a frown. "Sorry?"

"You're going to have a stranger living in the house with my son. Don't you think you should have asked me first?"

Indignation rose up inside her. "Like you asked me first when you moved in with Lisa? She was a stranger to Ollie, too, then. Remember?"

"That's hardly the same thing."

"No, it isn't, because I'm *having* to do this, where you just did it because you wanted to. I need the money. Ollie and I are struggling to get by, and you never help with any extras financially, so this is what it's come to."

Haiden chose that moment to come down the stairs. "Oh, hello." His expression faltered. "I'm not interrupting anything, am I?"

"No, not at all," she said with a forced smile. "Ollie, this is Haiden."

Ollie lifted his hand in a wave.

"Hello, Ollie." Haiden gave the boy a relaxed grin. "I see you like to play with Legos. You want to show me what you built?"

Ollie looked towards her with an unsure expression.

"It's okay," she encouraged him. "You can show him. I'll be right here."

Ollie nodded and bounded off, Haiden following. Already she could hear his chatter about the latest dragon Lego he'd just built, though she'd been the one to do most of the work.

Stephen grabbed Kristen's arm and pulled her out of the house and onto the front step.

"Hey!" she hissed. "Get your hands off of me!"

"What the hell do you think you're playing at?"

"What?"

"When you said you were taking in a foreign student, I thought you meant a teenager. That is a grown man!"

"I didn't want to have the responsibility of another child in the house. It is hard enough, it just being me and Ollie."

"But you don't know this man. How can you trust him around our son?"

"Oh, for goodness sake. The university checks the students out before housing them with people and not everyone is some kind of kiddy fiddler, you know. He seems like a genuine guy, and he's here to study, that's all. It'll be twelve weeks and then he'll go home again."

"And then you'll have someone else coming into our son's home?"

"Yes, that's how it works. Some will stay for more time, some will stay for less. It's no different than if I were to bring in a lodger, except I get paid a lot more money, and I don't have to feel like someone else has equal rights to my home."

"Our home. This is still half my house, remember. I should be able to say what goes on inside its walls."

"No, actually, you don't get to say anything. You gave up on that right when you walked out on us. If I was knocking down walls or building extensions, then yes, you get to have a say, but you don't get to have a say about this."

His lips thinned, and he folded his arms across his chest. "I'm not comfortable with this at all, Kristen."

"So, what are you going to do? You can help me out by increasing what you pay in child maintenance, or you could offer to have Ollie more regularly so I'm not having to pay for every meal."

He shuffled his feet, glancing at the ground. "It's not that easy. What with the business sucking every penny out of me, and the new baby as well... It was very stressful last night trying to get a whole heap of small children to stay in bed."

She barked laughter. "Stressful? You should try living my life for a few days. You should try feeding pasta to your child for three days in a row because that's all you've got until payday, or explaining to Ollie why his dad isn't showing up, yet again!" She'd managed to say all of this in a kind of hissed whisper, not wanting either Ollie or Haiden to hear their conversation. Stephen made her so mad, though. He was happy to criticise her but would never do anything to help.

"Look, Kristen. The truth is that things between me and Lisa have been pretty strained since the baby arrived. Our house isn't a fun place to be right now. No one is getting any sleep. Lisa is short-tempered with me all the time, and it doesn't help when Ollie is around. It just gives us something else to fight about."

She didn't want to experience a little buzz of pleasure that his new marriage was struggling, but she did.

"Sometimes," he continued, pausing to bite down on his lower lip, "I wonder if I made a mistake."

Her head shot up. "Oh, no. Don't you dare do that. You're several years too late. I don't want to hear it."

Where the hell had *that* come from? Was it just because he'd seen a tall, blond, gorgeous stranger in his ex-wife's home? Or was it because it was finally dawning on him that the grass wasn't always greener? It didn't matter either way. There was no chance she'd consider having him back. Life with him had been miserable.

Even if it's better for Ollie, her mother's voice sounded in her head. *Always thinking of yourself, Kristen. Such a selfish girl.*

She shook the thought away. She'd never been more miserable than when she'd been with Stephen. Sure, things were tough now, but she didn't spend every day questioning every little thing about herself, wondering if his excuses for coming home late at the weekend were true, and expecting every phone call to be from some woman who thought he was interested in her and had no idea he was married. He'd always come up with an excuse, calling her paranoid and crazy, and making her feel that way, too. He even brought up her mother and her sister, comparing her to them, making her doubt her own mind.

"Go back to your wife," she said, making her tone hard. "Mind your own business. And next time, make sure you show up for Ollie when you say you're going to."

Not waiting for his response, she stepped back into the house and quickly shut the door.

She leaned her back against it and exhaled a long, shaky sigh. Her hands were trembling, her stomach in knots. She hated confrontation, and confrontation with Stephen was the worst. He always seemed to know exactly how to push her buttons, sending her from calm to furious in a matter of seconds. She guessed it was because she still had so much invested in him. He'd always be Ollie's father, and Ollie was the most important person in her life, and that was never going to change.

As much as an infuriating arsehole as Stephen was, he wasn't going anywhere, and she just needed to get used to that.

Chapter Seven

Kristen was happy when Monday morning rolled around, and she could at least slip into a semblance of normality.

She pointed out the way to the bus to her new houseguest, making sure he knew which stop to get off at and that he had enough money to pay for the ride. He laughed her off, and she knew she was fussing around him like he was a child, but she didn't want to mess up, and besides, he was still in a strange country, however cool and easy he seemed to be with everything.

With Ollie happily ensconced at breakfast club, she went to the office to get the day started. Even though nothing happened at school over the weekend, somehow things still managed to build up, so she always ended up with a busy morning. Mondays tended to be the day where all the parents needed something, too. Letter slips were handed in, lunch meal tickets bought, enquiries about upcoming school trips made. There would be a barrage of phone calls from parents whose kids had fallen sick or injured themselves over the weekend and so wouldn't be making it to school that day.

Just as she sat down, Anna swept into the office. "Oh my God. I can't believe it's Monday already. I swear the weekend is at least three days too short."

"So, you want to swap the weekends for the weekdays?" she said with a smile.

"Yes, that sounds perfect! I'm never ready for it when Sunday night approaches. I always end up having one glass of wine too many and staying up too late watching movies on Netflix."

Kristen laughed, though she didn't know why Anna was complaining. She didn't have to work Mondays if she didn't want to. Her husband made enough for her to not need to work at all. But Anna said she got bored being home all day and wanted to feel like she was needed. It seemed kind of selfish to work a job she didn't really need, when someone else who needed the money could have worked it instead. Anna's time might have been better spent volunteering somewhere that really could have used an extra pair of hands. But Kristen wasn't going to tell her that. Really, it was none of her business what Anna chose to do with her life, and she had as much right to her own independence and feeling as though she was contributing to the household as anyone else.

"Well, I had an interesting weekend," she said.

Anna lifted her eyebrows. "You did?"

"Yeah. I got a placement from the university housing."

"Oh, wow. That was fast."

"It was a bit last minute, but it's all fine. The student is from Sweden and he's studying business. He seems very nice."

Anna narrowed her eyes at Kristen. "There's something else, isn't there? I can always tell when you're holding something back."

Kristen twisted her lips. "Well... he's a little older than I was expecting."

Anna frowned. "You asked for a mature student, didn't you?"

"True, I did, but I guess I was expecting someone who was eighteen. This guy is in his twenties."

She waggled her eyebrows. "So, you have a twenty-something Swedish guy living in your house?"

Kristen sighed. "Yeah, that was pretty much how Stephen's train of thought went, too, when he saw him."

"Stephen saw him? I guess he wasn't happy, then?"

"No. He said that he thinks he regrets us breaking up."

Anna let out a snort and rolled her eyes. "Jesus. What an arsehole."

"You got that right."

The school playground started to fill with parents and kids. The parents stood in small groups, while the children raced around with their friends at a million miles an hour. There was always the occasional child who didn't want to be back at school and cried while clinging to their mother or father's leg, but for the most part, the children were more than happy to be back. She kept an extra eye out for Ollie. The breakfast club kids were normally allowed five minutes in the playground before school started for real, letting them burn off some steam before they were expected to sit down and concentrate.

The line of parents needing things grew longer with every passing minute. Kristen forced her mind away from her son and focused on taking in permission slips and handing out lunch tickets. No matter how quickly she dealt with one person, another two seemed to take their place just as fast.

Suddenly, one of the older boys from year six came pushing through into the office. "Miss Scott, it's Ollie. He's got hurt and he's crying."

"What?" She was instantly on her feet. "What do you mean he got hurt? Did he fall over?" It wasn't unusual for Ollie to trip over. Like most five-year-old boys, he was always racing around and often fell over his own feet or ran into things.

"I don't know," the boy said.

She apologised to the waiting mums who waved her away, and then picked up her pace to half run into the playground. She could tell immediately where the incident had taken place. A little crowd of people had gathered around, and she pushed through them. "Sorry, excuse me. Sorry."

Her heart broke when she saw Ollie standing in the middle, tears pouring down his face. One of the other mums was comforting him and gave her a sympathetic smile as she approached.

"What happened?"

She caught a glimpse of Rachelle Hurst standing with her son, Felix, clutched against the front of her body. Felix was a year older than Ollie, and was known for being a troublemaker, but Rachelle was one of those mums who had a finger in every pie. She headed up the school's parent teacher association, and got involved with every fundraiser, making sure that she controlled exactly what everyone else was doing. She would wait by the front door and pounce to determine that you'd donated whatever it was they wanted for whatever the current fundraiser was—cakes, sweets, presents, sometimes even money. For someone like Kristen who struggled just making ends meet, the constant requests for donations were draining and embarrassing.

"What happened?" Kristen asked again.

Ollie was crying too hard to understand what he was saying, so she looked around at others for help.

Rachelle stepped forward. "I think the boys got into a bit of a tussle over the football. Ollie's just overreacting, that's all."

"What kind of a tussle?" She fixed her gaze on Felix, her over-protective side rising. "What did you do to Ollie?"

Rachelle's lips pinched. "Don't you talk to my son like that!"

"Then I suggest you ask him yourself. What's he done to make Ollie cry like this?"

Ollie tried to say something, and Kristen crouched to hear him better. "He bit my shoulder."

"What?"

Quickly, she pulled up the back of Ollie's shirt. Sure enough, there were already blue and purple bruises in the shape of a set of teeth.

"Jesus Christ." She glared at Felix. "You bit him?"

"He wouldn't let go of the ball," Felix muttered.

"Say sorry, Felix." Rachelle hissed through clenched teeth.

"Sorry," the boy said sulkily, looking away as though he was already bored.

Kristen straightened and shook her head. "I don't think 'sorry' is going to cut it. You can't have boys biting other boys—especially not when they're younger. This isn't the first time Felix has done something like this either. This needs to be dealt with properly."

Rachelle bristled. "I hope that's not a threat."

"No, me saying I was going to bite him back would be a threat," she spat, unsure where the words came from. "Animals bite. Are you an animal, Felix? Because you certainly behave like one."

Rachelle gasped in shock at her audacity.

"Come on, Ollie." Kristen took hold of her son's hand. "I think we need to speak with the headteacher."

She was horribly conscious of how everyone had stopped and were now staring as she marched her son through the playground towards the headteacher's office. This incident was bound to be the talk of the school.

She knocked on Andrew Larsen's door and waited for him to call to come in. She entered, still with a teary Ollie by her side, to find the headteacher sitting behind his desk.

"Andrew, I'm sorry, but I need to talk to you about Felix Hurst."

He sighed and put down his pen. "What's he done now?"

She pulled up the back of Ollie's shirt to show him. "He bit Ollie because Ollie wouldn't give him a football."

Andrew winced. "That looks sore." He frowned at her son. "You okay, Ollie?"

Ollie sniffed and nodded. "Yes, sir."

"Doesn't look as though the skin is broken," Andrew continued. "It's only bruised."

"It's a bite," she said, feeling as though he was missing the point. "You can't have kids biting other kids. They're not a bunch of animals."

"I understand that, Kristen. I'll be bringing Felix and his parents in and having a talk with them."

"I don't think having a talk with them is going to cut it. How many times is this boy going to injure another child before something is done? He pushed over one of the other boys last week, and nothing was done. Just because his mother is Rachelle Hurst doesn't mean he shouldn't be held to account for his actions."

His lips thinned. "What is that supposed to mean?"

"That you give the kid a free pass because his mum is head of the PTA."

"That's ridiculous, Kristen. I treat Felix just like every other child at this school."

Anger bubbled inside her, but she forced herself to push it down. She wanted to fight for her son's right to be able to come to school without fear of being bitten by another child, but she was also keenly aware that this was where both she and Ollie spent a large portion of their days.

"Are you okay, sweetheart?" she asked her still sniffling son. "Do you want to go home, or do you want to stay?"

Deep down, she prayed he wasn't going to ask to go home. There was already a big queue trailing out of the office door, and she knew Anna would be freaking out trying to deal with everyone. Besides, it would be a day of unpaid leave, and she couldn't afford to take that either.

"It's okay. I can stay," he said in a small voice.

Her heart broke. It was as though he'd seen straight into her head and decided to stay even though he probably didn't want to.

She gave him a hug. "That's my brave boy."

"Everyone will be going into class now, Ollie," the headteacher said. "I'll make sure I have a word with Felix so nothing like this happens again, okay?"

Ollie nodded again and turned to leave the office.

Kristen still didn't feel as though things were going to be dealt with severely enough, but what more could she do? She joined her son in the corridor outside. From the playground, one of the other teachers blew the whistle to signal it was time to go into class.

Kristen took Ollie back out into the playground so he could line up with the other children. She bent down and gave her son a kiss.

"I need to go back to the office now, Ollie, but you know where I am if you need me. If Felix does or says anything to you again, I want to know about it, okay?"

"Okay."

She glanced up and caught Rachelle glaring at her from the other side of the playground. Kristen pressed her lips together and stared back. She wasn't going to be intimidated by some bully's mother. Not when her son was involved.

Chapter Eight

S he was running late.

The bus should have already dropped Haiden off at the correct stop to deliver him back to the house shortly before five. It was just after that now, so she expected to find him sitting on the doorstep, which wasn't what she'd planned at all. She guessed she'd need to give him a key to the house at some point, but she hadn't had time to get one cut yet. It felt strange giving someone else the option to come and go whenever they pleased, even though it was well within Haiden's right to do so. The school imposed a curfew, but she guessed she could hardly force a man in his twenties to stick to it. It would be different if he was a teenager, but he wasn't.

Ollie seemed okay after the incident at school. He hadn't mentioned it since she'd picked him up from afterschool club, and she hadn't brought it up again herself. She was dreading bath time, though, knowing she was going to see those horrible bite marks again. She felt a fresh rush of protective anger at the thought. Bloody Felix. How would he like it if someone bigger started biting him?

She approached the house, but instead of finding Haiden waiting for them, something else caught her eye, and she drew to a halt. "Oh, no."

"What is it, Mummy?" Ollie asked from beside her.

"The plant pots are all broken!"

She did her best to keep the front of the house looking tidy. She always made sure Ollie's scooter and bike weren't left in the front garden, and she'd made the effort to have a couple of pretty, potted plants on either side of the front door. Now the plant pots were lying on their sides, the dirt and plants spilled onto the concrete path, the ceramic in fractured pieces.

"Did they get blown over?" Ollie asked doubtfully. She knew why he thought that—they'd had a storm over winter which had wrecked the garden and blown down a fence panel—but there hadn't been any wind today.

"I don't think so. Maybe someone knocked them over accidentally."

"Yeah, that was probably what happened," he agreed.

Movement came from behind them. "Hello."

She looked over her shoulder to see Haiden. He was all energetic youth and good health, and she felt ten years older and exhausted all at once.

"Oh, hi. I thought you would have been back by now."

"The bus was running late."

Lucky for her. "How was your first day?"

It felt strange asking someone that question when they were clearly nowhere near being a child.

He nodded. "It was good. Still getting my bearings, you know."

She smiled to show she did, but she'd left college at the age of eighteen with a couple of A-levels in dance and social studies to her name. She hadn't even done a degree, never mind a masters in something.

Haiden caught sight of what they were looking at and frowned. "Someone broke your pots."

His words jolted through her. Yes, that was what it looked like—as though someone had come along and deliberately knocked them over, so they broke, had maybe even picked them up and thrown them hard enough to smash. Her stomach twisted, hating the idea that someone would do that.

"I'm sure it was an accident. Let's get inside so I can get some food on. I don't know about the both of you, but I'm starving."

That was a lie. Her appetite had completely fled at the sight of the broken pots, but she needed to feed Ollie and Haiden.

"How does spaghetti bolognaise sound?"

She felt bad she was feeding them yet more pasta, but she'd found a packet of reduced mince in the discount aisle in the supermarket and could rustle up a fairly decent spag bol out of that and some basic canned tomatoes and a couple of other simple ingredients.

"Sounds great to me," Haiden said, giving her a smile, and something relaxed inside her.

"Spaghetti, yummy!" declared Ollie.

She laughed and pushed the front door shut behind them, closing herself off from the view of the mess outside. She'd need to clear them away so Ollie didn't go cutting himself on them, but she couldn't handle doing that now.

Instead, she went into the kitchen and busied herself with getting dinner started. The after-school club always gave Ollie a snack, but he was still ravenous by the time they got home. She wished she was able to pick him up at three-thirty and bring him home for dinner, just like a lot of the other mums did, but she needed to work. She could hear him now, making superhero fighting noises with his toys as he played in the living room.

Within minutes, she had the water boiling for the pasta, and the mince browning off in a pan. She'd throw in some onions, garlic, and celery, and then some tinned tomatoes and a stock cube for some extra flavour. It was a good, healthy meal and one she could rely on Ollie to eat heartily with no complaints.

She sensed someone behind her and glanced over her shoulder to find Haiden leaning against the kitchen doorframe.

"Oh, hi. I didn't know you were there. Can I get you a drink or something?"

"No, I'm fine, thanks." He straightened. "Please, tell me if I'm stepping out of line, but I'd like to go and clear up the mess while you're making dinner."

"I can't ask you to do that. You're a guest."

He shrugged. "I'm happy to do it. I'd rather help out than sit around feeling useless."

"You must have schoolwork to do."

"Nothing that won't wait until after dinner."

She exhaled a sigh of gratitude. "Thank you." She fished around under the sink for a dustpan and brush, and a carrier bag for him to put the broken ceramic in. "I really appreciate it."

"No problem," he said, flashing a set of white teeth.

She'd forgotten how good it felt to have someone else around to help with things. She'd been so used to doing everything on her own that she'd just accepted that was the way it was going to be. She watched his broad shoulders as he left the room, carrying the pan and carrier bag, and then turned back to the meal she was making. The sound of scraping and tinkling of broken porcelain filtered through to her from outside.

She didn't know who had broken the pots, but she could make some reasonable guesses. The worst part was that she wasn't going to be able to replace them any time soon. There was no way she could afford the extra money, though hopefully that would change over the next few weeks when the money from hosting would start to trickle in. There were more important things she needed to buy before worrying about pot plants, though, such as new clothes for Ollie, but hopefully she'd be able to siphon a little off to replace the pots eventually.

With the pasta and sauce ready, she dished it up into bowls, making sure Haiden and Ollie had the bigger portions. Haiden came in from outside and went to the sink to wash his hands.

"You have no idea who might have broken the pots, then?" he asked as she placed the bowls, together with knives and forks, on the small kitchen table.

"No, not really. I expect it was kids messing around. Maybe they kicked a football into the garden and knocked them down, and then grabbed the ball and ran off, not wanting to get in trouble."

"Hmm, maybe," he replied.

The pots hadn't looked like they'd just been knocked over, though. She thought to how angry Rachelle had been earlier, and also Stephen's reaction at finding Haiden here on Sunday morning. Would either of them stoop to something like that? Stephen had broken plenty of things when they were together and had been fighting. He'd put holes in the walls, and smashed picture frames, and had even ripped up a book she'd been reading when he'd wanted to get her attention. Maybe he'd come to try to see her, but when he discovered she wasn't in, he'd broken the pots in frustration, though she would have thought he'd have known she'd be at work. She should probably call him and demand he tell her the truth about it, but her stomach shrivelled at the thought of having to make any kind of contact with him that didn't involve arranging visiting times for Ollie.

"Thank you for cleaning up the mess, though," she told Haiden. "I really do appreciate it."

He flashed her that perfect white smile again. "No problem."

She called Ollie to the table, and they sat down to eat. Ollie wolfed down the first half of his meal then proceeded to talk non-stop at them both, telling them about every little thing that had happened at school, though he missed out the part about Felix biting him. Haiden joined in where he could, dropping in comments like 'wow' and 'no way' whenever Ollie took a breath long enough to allow anyone else to get a word in. Haiden had been right when he'd said he hadn't been a boy long ago either. He seemed to fit in easily around Ollie, and Ollie had warmed to him quickly.

A little ball of happiness swelled inside her at their company. Even though she knew it wasn't a permanent thing, it felt good to break up the monotony of it being just the two of them.

She tried not to let the image of the broken pots, Stephen's anger yesterday, or the teeth marks on Ollie's shoulder spoil her mood.

Chapter Nine

That evening, she sat on the closed lid of the toilet seat while Ollie took his bath. He played happily with the plastic bath toys, tipping liquid soaps and shampoos into various tubs and mixing them together to make potions. Each time she caught sight of the crescent moons of teeth marks in his shoulder, anger flashed bright through her.

This wasn't the first time Felix Hurst had been involved in something like this, and she knew it wouldn't be the last. He was known for picking on the other kids—especially ones smaller than he was. He'd shoved Ollie down the hill at school the term before, though he'd insisted it had been an accident when he'd been trying to get past, and Ollie had reluctantly agreed.

She was convinced if Felix had anyone else as a mother, things would have been dealt with far more strictly by now. Rachelle had far too much control over things at school. It wasn't as though she was any kind of governing official who'd been voted into her position. She was just another mother who had muscled her way into a job that no one else even wanted, and then used that job to intimidate and bully other parents. The problem was that she got the job done, and she raised critically needed funding for the school. With government budget cuts, teachers were struggling to have the most basic of provisions in class. The kids barely had glue sticks and colouring pens, never mind the bigger stuff like tablets and laptops for IT. Whatever she might think of Rachelle and her son, she did a good job of raising money to keep the classrooms supplied with those kinds of things, and no one wanted to upset her enough to make her no longer want to help.

Still, those teeth marks in Ollie's shoulder stirred a pot of anger inside Kristen.

She felt like biting Felix herself, so the kid knew exactly what it felt like. She didn't think he'd go around biting any more smaller kids if he knew someone bigger was going to come along and dish back to him exactly what he served out.

Immediately, she experienced a pang of remorse at the thought. She was an adult. A mother who worked at a school. She couldn't be thinking such things about one of the pupils. The boy was only six years old—almost seven—after all. He was still only a small child. No, the people she needed to be angry with were Rachelle and the headteacher—both for not coming down on Felix hard enough. They were all treating him as though he was just making mistakes, not being violent and assaulting another child. It was one thing his doing this kind of thing when he was six years old, but what would happen in a few years when he went to secondary school, and he got bigger and stronger? If someone didn't teach him right from wrong, he was going to end up in real trouble, and maybe even causing another person some permanent harm. They weren't doing the boy any favours by pandering to him.

"Ready to get out now, kiddo?" she said to Ollie when he'd been in the bath long enough. "You're turning into a prune."

Ollie laughed and held up his wrinkly fingers, and she pulled out the plug. Taking a towel off the rack, she half wrapped him in it and lifted him out of the bath. He was getting big now, and someday soon he'd be too heavy for her to be able to do this.

"Come on. Let's get you into some pyjamas."

She steered him out of the bathroom and towards his bedroom. They met Haiden on the landing as he was coming up the stairs, and she saw the student's gaze land on Ollie's shoulder, where it had become uncovered by the towel. He frowned slightly, and the idea that he might think she was responsible for the mark jolted through her.

"He got into a fight with an older boy at school," she explained quickly. "The boy bit him."

The lines in Haiden's forehead furrowed. "A boy bit him? Children shouldn't be treating each other like that at school."

She gave a tight smile. "That's what I said, too. The other mother wasn't happy with me, though. She thinks I'm over-protective, and that Ollie over-reacted."

Haiden gestured to the mark. "That clearly wasn't the case. You should always stand up for your son."

Warmth blossomed within her. It was nice to have someone around she could bounce things off, and not feel that she had to silently turn everything over in her head all evening.

"Thanks. I agree." She turned her attention to her son. "Come on, Ollie. PJs and then bed."

She stifled a yawn at the suggestion of bed. It had been a long day, and she didn't think she'd be far behind his bedtime either.

KRISTEN JERKED AWAKE, her heart racing.

Someone was in the room with her. *Ollie?*

She stared into the darkness, the only light the red glow from the LED clock. Pushing herself to sitting, she gasped. A male figure was standing at the end of her bed.

"Haiden?" She kept her voice low, just a hissed whisper, not wanting to wake Ollie—who was apparently still sleeping in his own bedroom. "What are you doing? What's wrong?"

But he didn't respond, and instead remained standing in the same position, looking down at her on the bed. His chest was bare, and all he wore was a pair of boxer shorts. She gathered the duvet around her, huddling the sheets closer to her chest. Did he know what he was doing? He must be sleepwalking. She'd found Ollie sleepwalking on a number of occasions, more often than not lurking around in the hallway after trying to find the toilet, but he'd always been at least a little responsive, answering her questions, even if the answers didn't always make sense.

It was eerie seeing Haiden like this, just standing there, staring down at her. Cold prickles of goose bumps rose across her arms, even though she was still snug in bed. She couldn't just leave him there. She was going to need to try to get him back to bed.

A fresh trickle of worry went through her. He was over six feet tall, and if he put up some kind of a fight and didn't know what he was doing, he might accidentally hurt her. She'd hate for that to happen, especially if it woke Ollie, and he was to find her, and then try to deal with Haiden.

No, she was overthinking things. The man was just asleep. There was no reason to think he'd hurt her in any way.

She was glad she'd started wearing a little more to bed now that she had Haiden living with them. Previously, she would have just slept in an old t-shirt and knickers, but she'd taken to wearing a pair of jersey shorts as well. Not that she thought Haiden would have any idea what she was wearing right now—he didn't even seem to know where he was.

Kristen threw back the bedcovers and climbed out of bed, all the instructions she'd heard over the years about how to deal with sleepwalkers running through her head. It was important not to startle him or try to wake him; she remembered that much, at least. She just needed to gently coax him back to bed.

"Haiden?" she said again, keeping her voice soft. "You're in the wrong room. Shall we get you back to bed now?"

He still didn't respond, so she reached out and touched his arm.

That got his attention. His head jerked towards her, and she gasped and stepped back. It was the suddenness of the movement that had made her jump. He was still staring at her, but she had the feeling he wasn't seeing her at all. Kristen let out a shaky breath. She didn't know why this was freaking her out so badly. It was only Haiden.

She tried again, putting on the cheerful singsong voice she used when she was trying to coax Ollie back to bed. "Come on, Haiden. Let's get you back to bed."

Something had got through to him, as he finally took a step.

"That's right. This way." She shuffled backwards, not wanting to turn her back on him. She was tempted to take his hand to try to lead him, but she didn't want to touch him.

He kept coming, however, and she was able to exhale a sigh of relief as she guided him down the hallway and to the spare room that was now his bedroom. She stood out of the way as he pushed past her and got back into bed, curling up on his side.

Cautiously, she reached over and pulled up the duvet, covering his bare shoulders. She remained standing over him—their positions reversed—watching and waiting to make sure he wasn't going to get out of bed again. But his breathing had slowed, his shoulders gently rising and falling, and she was sure he was fully asleep once more.

She backed out of the room and gently closed the door behind her.

Well, that had been weird.

She went back to her bed and climbed back into the spot she'd vacated, the mattress and blankets still warm. It was quarter past three now, and her heart was still racing from the strange experience. She wasn't sure she was going to get back to sleep again, and she dreaded the thought of the next day and trying to function at work.

Was Haiden a chronic sleepwalker? She felt sure it was something that should have been mentioned to her. Though she felt kind of awkward about it, she was going to have to bring it up with him in the morning. She needed to know if this was going to be a regular occurrence—not that she could do much about it, of course. She dreaded the idea of lying awake every night, anticipating the creak of the landing floorboards as a heavy male foot pressed down on them. Him coming into her bedroom, rather than anywhere else in the house, was strange, too. Had his subconscious told him to come in here for some reason? She guessed it was better than him having gone into Ollie's room. It would have frightened the little boy, and at least she was better equipped to deal with it.

Tossing and turning, she willed her mind to shut off, but now she was worrying about Ollie and the incident at school with Felix. That wasn't something that was just going to go away either. Unless they had the good fortune of Rachelle moving to a different area, and Felix changing schools, they were going to be spending every day together for the next five years. And she didn't want to change schools either. They were really lucky to be in the catchment area they were in. Despite her being pregnant when they'd bought the house, she and Stephen hadn't even considered school in the local area because that had all felt so far away. It was sheer luck that meant Ollie automatically got to go to a lovely little school on the outskirts of town. Plus, her job was there, and they were able to walk every day.

Having to change schools just because of one bully didn't seem fair at all.

Chapter Ten

The following morning, she was foggy-headed due to lack of sleep, barely focusing as she set out the cereal and milk for breakfast. She'd tossed and turned for a good hour and had last seen the clock at five a.m. before she'd eventually got back to sleep. Then, before she felt like she'd slept at all, her alarm went off at seven.

That had definitely not been a good night's sleep, and she hoped Haiden wasn't going to make a habit of sleepwalking. It was hard enough having a five-year-old who liked to creep into her bed in the middle of the night, without worrying about a grown man. The whole point of having an adult here instead of a child was that she hadn't wanted to worry about the responsibility of looking after them.

Ollie emerged into the kitchen, all tousled hair and sleepy eyes, still wearing his batman pyjamas.

"Good morning, kiddo," she said, trying to make her voice bright so he couldn't see how tired she was. She didn't want him to worry. "Sleep well?"

"Uh-huh," he replied, automatically walking up to her so she could give him a hug, pressing him to her body and kissing the top of his head. He might have lost that wonderful baby smell a long time ago, but she still loved how he smelled after he'd been sleeping.

"Good." She released him. "Now go and sit down, and help yourself to some cereal, and I'll put some toast on for you."

"Will you pour the milk?"

"Of course, I will."

She put the bread in the toaster and set about finishing making her tea, and she made a cup for Haiden as well. She was going to have to mainline caffeine today if she was going to make it through. Creaking from upstairs, and the sound of the toilet flushing, let her know that her houseguest was up. She poured the milk onto Ollie's chocolate hoops and added some to the brewing tea as well.

"Mummy, the toast is burning!" Ollie suddenly exclaimed.

Black smoke poured from the top of the toaster, and the smoke alarms went off with a shrill beep.

"Shit!"

"Mummy!" he said, aghast. "That's a swear word."

She fished the charcoaled pieces of toast out of the toaster and threw them into the sink. "I know, I know. I'm sorry."

Damn. She must have pushed the toast down for a second time, thinking it was bread she still needed to toast.

Heavy footsteps thundered down the stairs, and Haiden, appearing as fresh faced and youthful as ever, stepped into the kitchen.

"Does that mean breakfast is ready?" he said with a grin, pointing into the air, clearly meaning the smoke alarm.

She forced herself to smile and tried not to feel resentful at the fact the reason she was so exhausted was because of him.

"Ha ha," she said, deadpanning, and then handed him a tea towel. "The smoke alarm is out in the hallway. Will you waft this under it? Get some fresh air around it until the beeping stops."

"Sure."

He vanished again, and she set about opening the windows and then putting some fresh bread into the toaster. She really couldn't afford to be throwing food away like this.

The alarm finally went off, and she exhaled a sigh of relief, her shoulders dropping.

"There, all fixed," Haiden said, reappearing.

"Thanks. Sit down and have some breakfast."

She finished making fresh toast and offered some tea and juice to Haiden as well.

"Go on upstairs and brush your teeth," she told Ollie when he'd finished eating, "and find your school shoes, too."

"Can't I watch some TV first?" he whined.

"No. You know you don't get to watch TV during the week." If she let him, he'd be sitting there, staring at the screen and getting nothing done until well after school had started.

He pouted but hopped up and ran upstairs.

"Well, that was an exciting start to the morning," Haiden said with that easy grin of his. It was hard to believe this was the same person who'd been staring at her in bed, cold and expressionless, at three in the morning.

Butterflies flipped in her stomach at the idea of mentioning it to him, but she knew she was going to have to. She couldn't just say nothing.

"Speaking of exciting starts," she said, "do you remember coming into my room last night?"

His mouth dropped open. "What?"

"Yeah, I think you were sleepwalking. I woke up and you were standing over the bed."

His expression changed, his features growing hard. "I don't know what you're talking about. I don't sleepwalk."

Her stomach dropped. She'd hoped they'd have been able to laugh about it and smooth things over, but it didn't seem as though Haiden was going to let her do that. His hackles had come up, and he was clearly defensive, though she couldn't think why.

"Umm, I'm afraid you do. You were definitely sleepwalking last night. It's perfectly normal. It's probably just because of the strange surroundings, and the new start at university. All kinds of pressures can make someone sleepwalk, even if they've never done it before, or at least been unaware that they've been doing it."

His blue eyes narrowed. "I told you, I don't sleepwalk. I never have, and I have no memory of doing so last night. Isn't there as much of a chance that you dreamed the whole thing."

His words hit her like a cannonball. She'd never even considered that he might deny what had happened and try to turn it around on her. "What? No! That's ridiculous. I'm exhausted because I barely slept last night because I was putting you back to bed. I definitely didn't dream it."

"Well, I definitely didn't sleepwalk, so I guess it's just a matter of one person's word against the other." He put down the piece of toast he'd been eating. "I'm going to be late for the bus, so I suggest we just drop the subject."

She stood in the middle of the kitchen, shocked into silence, as he got to his feet and left the room. A minute later, the front door slammed, and she jumped, her hand clutched to her chest. What the hell had just happened? His reaction had been the last thing she'd been expecting. Did he really think he hadn't sleepwalked, and she'd dreamed the whole thing? The idea was ludicrous. But why would he get so defensive about it? It wasn't as though it was something to be ashamed of. He hadn't done it on purpose.

Ollie reappeared, his shoes actually on his feet. "I brushed my teeth, Mummy."

"Good boy."

He looked around. "Did Haiden leave for school already?"

"Yeah, he needed to get in early today."

She had no idea if that was true or not, but it felt more like he'd left early to avoid her.

With a sigh, she finished her tea, only to get down to the bottom of the cup and discover the teabag lurking at the base. It wasn't even eight a.m. yet and she could already tell it was going to be one of those days.

Chapter Eleven

K risten got home after work that evening to find Haiden standing on the doorstep, a bunch of tulips in his hand.

"I'm really sorry about what happened this morning," he said. "I don't know why I acted like I did. Of course, if you say I was sleepwalking, then I must have been sleepwalking. And I'm sorry for disturbing your sleep, too. I'll try not to let it happen again."

She sagged with relief. After a tense day at work, having to drag herself through it due to lack of sleep, and making mistakes at every turn, the idea of being in a fraught atmosphere at home had stressed her out, too.

"That's okay. It was a bit of a shock, perhaps?"

"I was embarrassed, too," he admitted. "I didn't like the idea of you catching me in only my underwear. I'd normally make a bit more of an effort the first time a woman sees me half naked."

Her cheeks bloomed with warmth at the memory of his half-naked, tanned, muscular torso. There wasn't an ounce of fat on him. "I didn't look, I promise. I just got you straight back to bed, same as I'd have done with Ollie."

She blushed again, not wanting him to think of her as his mother, either.

He pushed the flowers at her. "These are for you to say sorry."

"You didn't need to get me anything," she said, accepting the flowers. She couldn't remember the last time anyone had bought her flowers—probably one of the times when Stephen had been caught eyeing up another woman. What was it with men, and apologetic flowers, and more annoyingly, why did they work to smooth things over, as though she could be bought with some pretty blooms?

But this time it did work, and she was happy to accept them. Even more happy that it meant they weren't going to be angry or awkward with each other anymore. She didn't know Haiden well enough to be trying to exist in that kind of atmosphere.

"And please, tell me if I do it again," he added. "I'll see if there's something I can do to help—hypnosis, maybe... I don't know." He shook his head and ran his hand through his blond hair. "But I promise not to act all crazy on you again if you tell me."

She smiled. "Deal."

"Anyway," he shouldered his bag full of books, "I'd better go up to my room and get some work done. Seems they were taking it easy on us for the first few days."

"Of course. I'll call you when dinner is ready."

Later, when the food was ready, they ate with an easy companionship, the tension from the previous night already blown over. Ollie seemed to enjoy Haiden's company, too, and Haiden was happy to join in with the hundred and one questions Ollie asked.

"What's been your favourite part of the day?" the boy asked both of the adults. Kristen smiled. This was a regular thing her son asked, and normally it was just the two of them. "Mine was scoring a goal against Sammy Benz at lunchtime."

Kristen joined in. "Mine was picking you up and finding out about your amazing goal scoring at lunchtime."

Ollie beamed back at her. "And what was yours?" he asked Haiden.

"Hmm." Haiden rubbed his fingers against his lips. "I'd have to say right now, sitting here with you both and eating this delicious meal."

Kristen flushed hot at the compliment, the warmth spreading inside her. It definitely was a good part of the day—perhaps even her favourite, though she wouldn't tell Ollie that.

Once they'd finished eating, Haiden helped her clear away the dishes, and then told her he was going to go to his room to get some work done.

"Of course. I'll make sure Ollie doesn't disturb you."

She had a ton of chores that needed finishing, anyway. The laundry pile was something that never came to an end, and right now it seemed larger than ever. She could handle the washing and the drying part, but for some reason, folding and putting it away drove her crazy.

With piles of folded laundry balanced in her arms, she carried the clothes upstairs to be put away.

She paused outside of Haiden's room, sensing him in there.

A buzzing sound filtered through to her from behind the closed door. *Buzz... pause... buzz..... Pause...* She recognised the noise but was unable to place it for a moment. And then it came to her—of course, it was a phone ringing with the sound off.

She frowned. Who was calling him, and why didn't he want to answer? She knew he was in there, so he must be right next to the phone. Perhaps it was just a sales call about something, and he was letting it ring out. Not that it was any of her business.

Going into Ollie's room, she spotted the boy lying on his bed, running toy cars over the mound of his pillow and into a gully of his duvet, which he'd pushed together to create a makeshift racetrack.

"Hey, kiddo," she said as she put his clothes away in his chest of drawers. "Time to get ready for bed. PJs on."

"Ooh, Mum!" he whined, throwing himself dramatically onto his back. "It's too early to go to bed yet!"

"No, it isn't. It's exactly your bedtime. Same as any other school night."

"Fine," he said, punching the pillow and then getting to his feet.

He pulled his t-shirt up over his head.

Kristen's mouth dropped open. "Oh, my God, Ollie. How did you get that bruise?"

A massive blue and purple splodge covered his skinny little ribs. Ollie clamped his arms down to his sides and looked away. "I don't know."

"Yes, you do. There's no way you could get that kind of bruise and not know where it came from."

"I said I don't know!" he yelled, and she started back. It wasn't like Ollie to shout.

He pushed past her, trying to get out of the room, but she caught him by the arm.

"Let me go." He wriggled in her grip.

"Not until you tell me where that bruise came from. I mean it, Ollie. It's important you tell me what's going on with you. Did someone do this to you?"

Felix Hurst. The name jumped into her head, but she managed to keep it from spilling from her mouth. She didn't want to give Ollie ideas. He might have hurt himself on the play equipment at school, but then she didn't know why he wouldn't just tell her that.

The boy remained with his lips clamped shut.

"Ollie, baby. I'm not mad with you, okay?" she said, pulling the little boy onto her lap, so they were both sitting on the edge of his bed. "But if someone has been hurting you, then you need to tell me. This is not all right. No one is allowed to touch you, do you understand?"

His body had been stiff against hers, but now he relaxed a fraction.

"Did someone tell you that you weren't allowed to say who hurt you?"

Ollie nodded against her shoulder, and anger speared through her.

"Did they tell you that you'd get in trouble if you told?"

Again, Ollie nodded.

Kristen stroked his hair and gritted her teeth. There was no doubt in her mind that Felix Hurst was responsible for hurting Ollie. That little shit must have punched or kicked her baby in the ribs, and then when he saw how much he'd hurt the other boy, he'd threatened Ollie not to say anything. This had to stop. If an adult had bruised another adult like this, and also put teeth marks into someone's shoulder, they'd have had a pretty good case for actual bodily harm. Just because this was two children involved shouldn't make it any less serious.

Despite knowing what she had to do, her stomach knotted at the thought of going into school the next day. It was difficult when her work situation was so closely blended with Ollie's school life. And she knew the headteacher and Felix's mother were friendly. She was sure she couldn't have been the only parent to complain about Felix's behaviour, however. Maybe she should ask around a bit first and see if she could find some other parents who would back her up. Although she was also aware that this might get her into trouble for starting rumours.

She let out a sigh and nuzzled her nose into her son's soft, fine hair. This was definitely a tricky situation. But she needed to put Ollie first. No matter what the consequences.

Chapter Twelve

"Andrew, can I have a word?"

The headteacher looked up from his work. "Kristen, of course. How can I help you?"

She sidled into his office and shut the door behind her. He gestured to the seat on the opposite side of his desk and she plopped herself down.

"I'm concerned about Ollie and how things are with Felix Hurst. I found a massive bruise on Ollie's ribs last night. Combined with the teeth marks on his shoulder, my poor boy looks like he's being beaten up. I'm really not happy."

Andrew sighed and dropped his pen on the desk. He sat back in his chair and steepled his fingers against his lips. "Look, Kristen, we both know how boys can be. They tend to rough and tumble, and sometimes that does result in bumps and bruises."

She raised her eyebrows in disbelief. "And in teeth marks? I don't think so. And it's not as though this is a joint thing, is it? I mean, Felix isn't sitting in here with bruises that Ollie has given him. The boy is bigger and stronger, and whether or not it's done deliberately, it shouldn't be happening."

He gave a long sigh, and Kristen bristled. He made her feel as though she was making a fuss about nothing and wasting his time.

"You know I've already spoken to both Felix and his mother about what happened with the biting incident, so I think we need to shelve that for the moment. As for the bruises, I'll get both boys in here today and sit down and have a little chat. If they can't play nicely together, I'll suggest they give each other some space. This isn't a big school, but it's big enough for them both to play in different areas."

"This isn't about two kids not playing nicely. This is about one bigger, older kid being physically violent towards a younger one."

Her mouth had run dry, her hands clenched to fists in her lap. Why was he struggling to see the truth of this? Was he deliberately being obtuse? She forced herself to take a breath, trying to calm herself down. It wouldn't do Ollie any good if she lost her temper. But this was all so frustrating.

"Look," she said, loosening her fingers and dropping her shoulders down, "if these were two adults, and one had left marks on another like that, there would be some serious questions asked."

He leaned forward in his seat. "Yes, but they're not adults. Just like you wouldn't expect a child to be tried as an adult in court, you can't expect the same thing to happen here. Children aren't expected to think of the consequences of their actions like an adult would. Their brains aren't developed enough yet."

"Which is why we as the adults need to teach them!"

"And that's exactly what I'm trying to do here, Kristen. Let me get the boys in and speak to them. I'm not saying that Ollie has done anything wrong, but it's also good for Felix to see how his actions have affected others."

She wanted to tell him how she felt this would all be handled a lot differently if it wasn't Rachelle Hurst's son who was causing all the problems. That woman lorded it over this school, and even the headmaster was afraid of her. It was pathetic. She wished she could go and tell Rachelle exactly what she thought of her and her son, but she knew it would only get her in trouble, and it wouldn't do any good, anyway. Rachelle thought the sun shined out of Felix's backside and would never believe that he was the nasty little bully he was.

Instead, she pushed back her seat and got to her feet. "Okay. Will you let me know how it goes?"

He nodded. "Of course."

Deflated, Kristen went back to her office. Anna looked up from her computer as she walked in and gave her a sympathetic smile.

"How did it go?"

"As expected."

She sank down into her seat and tried to focus on her work, while constantly having one eye out for Ollie. It was fine while he was in class and safe away from Felix Hurst, but at breaktimes and lunchtime, her anxiety rocketed, worried that her baby was being hurt.

The end of the school day finally arrived, and Kristen went to pick Ollie up from afterschool club and walk him home. She deliberately didn't mention Felix, allowing Ollie the chance to bring it up, but he didn't. He didn't even mention the headteacher bringing the two of them in for a chat, and she hadn't seen anything. True, she'd been busy most of the day, shut away in the office, so it wasn't as though she saw everyone who came and went from Andrew's office. Still, doubts ran through her.

"Did Mr Larsen have a chat with you and Felix today about that bruise you got?"

He looked up at her, his eyes wide. "No. You didn't tell on Felix, did you, Mummy?"

"I had to say something, sweetheart. I'm your mum, and it's my job to make sure you're safe."

"I don't want to get in more trouble."

She stopped, pulling him to a halt with her, and crouched to his level. "You're not in trouble. Not even one little bit, okay?"

He pressed his lips together and nodded, but she could see he was worried, and it broke her heart. Fucking Felix.

She rose to standing again, and together they walked back to the house. As she approached the gate, she saw something and let out a little 'oh' of surprise.

Ollie had noticed it, too. "Your pots are back together!"

Her mouth dropped open, and she stepped into her front garden, taking in the sight of the pretty plant pots with the bedding plants of pinks and whites and yellows spilling out of them.

Movement came at the side of the house, and Haiden walked around from the back yard, brushing his hands off on the backs of his jeans. He stopped short when he saw her standing there.

"Oh, hi."

"Did you do this?" she asked.

He shrugged, and gave a half smile, his cheeks pinkening in a way that was nothing short of adorable. "It's nothing, really."

"It's not nothing. I can't remember the last time someone did something so nice for me." Stupidly, after her stressful day, and the worries about Ollie and Felix, she found her eyes filling with tears. She pinched her lips and shook her head, trying to hold herself off from crying.

"Are you okay?" he asked, quickly stepping forward, touching her elbow with the tips of his fingers. "I didn't mean to upset you."

"No, you didn't, honestly. There's just been some stuff going on at school with that boy not being very nice to Ollie, and I've been stressing out about it all. This is such a lovely surprise that you've made me a little emotional."

"It shouldn't be that way, Kristen," he said, lifting his blue gaze to hers. "You should have people in your life who want to do nice things for you."

She glanced away, embarrassed. "It's just me and Ollie, really. And I'm okay with that, most of the time."

She couldn't allow herself to get used to having him around. It was a dangerous route to go down. They were already a week into his twelve-week stay, and once those twelve weeks were up, he would go back to his life in Sweden. Then she would have someone different come and live with her, and that person could be a whole different experience to how Haiden was.

Trouble was, she already thought she was going to miss him when he was gone.

Chapter Thirteen

Kristen bent to scoop the mail off the front mat. She never liked picking up the post. There was never anything good in it, always just more bills or bank statements telling her how low her funds were.

She rifled through the letters and paused at one. It didn't look like all the others. It was written on a plain white envelope, rather than one with that little cellophane see-through window or with the stamp of a utility company or something recognisable on it.

With her heart fluttering, she quickly tore open the letter. Better to get these things done and out of the way than to ignore it and hope it just went away. It never did. She pulled out the letter and frowned down, recognising the header. It was the solicitors Stephen had used during their divorce settlement. She'd seen that letter header often enough over the last few years. What the hell could they be writing to her about now? Everything had been settled during the divorce. Quickly, she scanned the contents of the letter. *What the fuck?*

The words hit her like a bolt to the heart, and her mouth dropped open. Due to a change in circumstances, Stephen was requesting to change the access set up. It read that he was no longer comfortable with Ollie spending as much time in her home and that he was seeking longer access hours.

In disbelief, Kristen barked out laughter. How the fuck did Stephen think he had the rights to longer access hours when he didn't even show up for the ones he currently had? She shook with anger. This was all about Haiden staying here, she didn't doubt it. And her rebuttal of Stephen's hints that he wanted to get back together the other day probably hadn't helped. He had no intention of spending more time with Ollie—she would have encouraged it if he had. No, this was all about upsetting her and making sure she knew her place.

Though she wanted to screw up the letter and throw it in Stephen's face, she knew she needed to keep hold of any paperwork. This was about protecting her and Ollie as much as anything else. She stormed into the kitchen where she'd left her mobile phone on the side and snatched it up. With a shaking hand, she pulled up Stephen's number and hit the call button.

Within two rings, he answered. "So, I assume you got the letter from my solicitor?"

She didn't miss the smug tone to his voice. "Yes, I did, and you can shove it where the sun doesn't shine. I mean, how fucking ridiculous can you get? You don't even show up when you're supposed to have him, and now you're expecting to see Ollie more often. You are having a laugh. What you're basically asking for is more opportunities to let our son down."

"That's not it at all," he said. "I've spoken to Lisa, and she's agreed that it might be easier if Ollie is here more often. That way he'll get used to being in his bed here, and things won't be so difficult."

She laughed again. "Oh, is this the same Lisa that you said to me the other week you were having second thoughts about?

The same Lisa you now have a baby with and who you were thinking of dumping to come running back to me?"

"That's not what I said at all." His voice was sharp. "You're twisting things around. Making them up in your head, just like you always did."

"Don't try to bullshit me, Stephen," she snapped. "I'm not susceptible to your little games anymore. And I never twisted things around in my head all those years ago. I was paranoid for a fucking good reason. You were sleeping around on me the entire time I was stuck at home with a new baby, feeling shit about myself."

They'd had this argument so many times, she didn't even know why she was letting the words come out of her mouth. The fight wouldn't make any difference. He would always make her think everything was her fault. And it wasn't as though she even wanted him back. He could keep his cheating self to himself.

"Actually," she said, "I feel sorry for Lisa, because I was her once upon a time, and I know exactly how it feels to have a new baby and have you eyeing up other women who look like better options."

Stephen laughed. "See, you're making things up in your head again. I'm not doing any of those things. Lisa is perfectly fine and happy."

She snorted down the phone. "That's not what you said to me when you dropped Ollie off on Sunday. We both know the only reason we're having this conversation is because you saw Haiden here. This has nothing to do with Ollie and everything to do with you not liking the thought of another man living here."

"Too damned right, I don't. We don't know anything about him."

"Yes, we do. He's been vetted by the university housing. And he's good with Ollie, too. But even if he wasn't, this is still none of your business. I have parental responsibility over Ollie, and unless there was some real reason why another man couldn't live here, then I could have as many men living here as I choose. This is my life, Stephen, not yours. You've gone off and lived yours, however the hell you wanted, without consulting me once, so don't think you get to say what happens in my life."

She stopped and took a shuddery breath, her hand on the kitchen worktop to steady herself. She needed to remember this all affected Ollie as well. He was always going to be number one to her, even above her own emotions, and she needed to think of that now.

"Listen to me, Stephen. If you genuinely want to see Ollie more often, I'm not going to stand in the way of that. You're his dad, and that will never change. I never want to be the kind of mother who gets in between the son and his father simply because I think the father is a piece of shit."

She heard Stephen's sharp breath. "That's a bit harsh, Kristen, don't you think?"

"Actually, no, I don't," she replied, "but here we are. If you want to start having him every weekend instead of every other weekend, then we can work with that. But you turn up when you say you're going to, and you don't let him down."

There was silence on the other end.

"Stephen? Are you still there?"

"Yeah, I'm here." His tone had grown hard. "So, what you're saying is you want Ollie out of the house every weekend."

Kristen gaped. "No, I'm saying this in response to the letter you sent me from your solicitor. You said you wanted Ollie more often."

"Yes, but not just so you can have private time with a boy young enough to be your son."

She laughed at the absurdity of his words. "Haiden is in his twenties. I would have been a child myself if I'd had him." Kristen tried to bring herself back to the topic at hand. This wasn't about Haiden. This was about access to Ollie. She took another breath and tried again. "If you don't want Ollie at the weekends, are you saying you want him during the week? That would be crazy. You live on the other side of the city and have to get another child to school and get to work yourself. How do you plan to get Ollie into school as well?"

"He could always change schools. He could go to the local one with Lisa's daughter."

"And then when am I supposed to see him?"

"Maybe you should be the one who has him at the weekends."

She felt like someone had just ripped out her guts. He was talking about Ollie mainly living with him and Lisa. She didn't want that at all. The idea of spending all week without Ollie was heart-breaking—not getting up in the morning and making his packed lunch, and getting his little school uniform on, and kissing him goodbye when she dropped him off at breakfast club. The thought broke her heart.

"I'm not having this conversation with you anymore, Stephen," she said curtly. "I'm not going to uproot Ollie just because you're jealous of a student staying here. He'll be gone in a few weeks, anyway, and then what are you going to do? Just move Ollie back here again? This whole thing is ridiculous."

Her hand was shaking as she ended the call. Trembling with adrenaline and sick at the idea of losing her son, she stared down at the phone in hatred. With a scream, she threw the phone down. "You fucking bastard!"

She winced at the crack of the phone hitting the floor. She'd thrown it too hard. Picking the phone back up, she saw the screen was cracked, and it had turned itself off. *Shit, shit, shit.* She couldn't afford to have a broken phone right now.

Kristen pressed the button to turn the phone back on again, and miraculously, the screen flashed to life.

She exhaled a sigh of relief. There was nothing she could do about the crack, but at least it was still working. For the time being, anyway.

Chapter Fourteen

"Nancy!" she exclaimed as she opened the door to find the woman from the university housing on her doorstep.

Haiden was staying late at the university that day, so wasn't back as normal. Kristen had finally got around to getting him a key cut so he could come and go as he wanted.

She frowned, suddenly worried. "Is everything all right?"

"Yes, fine. I'm sorry to just turn up like this. I wanted to have a quick chat and see how you were getting on. I'm aware this is your first student stay."

"Oh, of course. Come on in. Would you like a cup of tea?"

"Yes, please. That would be lovely."

Kristen led her through into the kitchen. She was aware of how Nancy was glancing around, taking in everything. Was she suspicious of something? Heat crept up Kristen's chest as she thought of the moments with Haiden where she'd felt like something had passed between them. Had Haiden said something to the student housing about her? Had she done something inappropriate and now Nancy was here to have a little chat with her? God, she would be mortified.

Trying to hide her discomfort, she went to the kettle and busied herself with filling it with fresh water and taking cups down from the cupboard.

She couldn't put it off any longer. The suspense was killing her.

"So," she said, turning to face Nancy, "what sort of things did you want to chat about?"

She forced a smile and wished she didn't feel so God-damned guilty. It wasn't as though she'd done anything wrong, had she?

"I did have a reason for coming here, actually," Nancy replied.

Kristen's mouth ran dry, her pulse racing. "Oh?"

She quickly turned and took the teabags out of the mugs and stirred in a little milk. Hoping her hands weren't shaking, she picked up the mugs and carried them over to the table and set them both down.

"I didn't want to look like I'm interfering," Nancy continued, pulling the cup of tea towards her, "since Haiden is a grown man and can do whatever he wishes, within reason, but I just wondered if he'd mentioned falling out with his parents."

Kristen frowned. "His parents? No, not at all. In fact, he says they're close."

Nancy pursed her lips. "Hmm. Yes, that's what they told me, too. I probably shouldn't even be getting involved, considering he's twenty-three years old, and family issues really shouldn't be a part of our concern. But of course, things like this can affect a student's ability to concentrate."

She lifted a hand to stop the other woman. "I'm sorry, but I think I'm missing something. Things like what, exactly?"

"Oh, it's probably nothing, but Haiden's mother emailed the office to say she hasn't managed to speak with Haiden since he left. He's sent them text messages to let them know he's fine and everything is going well, but whenever she tries to call, he never answers, and he's made no attempt to call home either."

"Right... that's strange."

A wave of relief washed over her. This wasn't anything to do with something she might have done or said.

"I mean," Kristen continued in a rush, "I've heard his mobile phone ringing on occasions, but I didn't really think anything of it. Maybe he's just really busy and hasn't had time to talk."

Lines appeared between Nancy's eyebrows, and she pressed her lips together. "That is what I told his mother as well, but she insisted it was really out of character for him not to call and speak to them all." She threw her hands up in the air. "But there's nothing we can do about it. If he doesn't want to speak to his mother, it's not like we can force him. He's not a child."

Kristen pulled a face. "Sorry I can't be of more help."

"You've been more than helpful. It's not as though we expect you to get involved with the personal lives of the students, though obviously, if you have any concerns, then don't hesitate to contact us." She leaned in closer, her head tilted slightly to one side. "You don't have any concerns, do you?"

"No, none at all. Haiden's been a pleasure to have around." She clamped her mouth shut, not wanting to say anything more. She didn't want to say the wrong thing and ruin everything. If she said he stayed up in his room all the time, and didn't get involved with their family life, they might think him to be overly withdrawn and that she hadn't made enough of an effort to get him involved. But if she told the truth about how it felt like they'd become their own little family in the matter of a week, and that she was already dreading him going, she didn't think that would go down too well either.

"Right, well, I'd better be off," Nancy said. "If you do hear anything you think we might need to know about, please, just give me a call."

Kristen noticed how she'd barely touched her tea, the drink still steaming hot. "Sure." She thought of something. "Should I mention to Haiden that you were here? Or that his parents want to hear from him?"

Nancy flapped a hand, the blue nail varnish on her nails chipped and tatty. "No, no need. We wouldn't want him to think we were spying on him, and we've already let him know his parents want to hear from him. Hopefully, he'll just pick up the phone and everyone can stop worrying."

She hadn't been worrying, but now she wondered if perhaps she should be. What possible reason could Haiden have for not wanting to speak to his folks? Not that it was any of her business, of course. She hoped Ollie would still want to speak to her in twenty years, when he was fully grown and off doing exciting things. Her mind flashed forward twenty years, and the idea of a woman in her thirties who already had a son and an ex-husband having her eye on Ollie jumped into her head. She'd be furious and would make sure the other woman knew to keep her hands off her boy. Could that be part of the reason Haiden hadn't called his family. Did she have something to do with it?

SHE WAS RELIEVED WHEN the working week came to an end.

To her surprise, Stephen came to pick up Ollie, stating that he'd have him for an extra night this weekend considering he'd missed the Friday night the week before. Ollie seemed happy enough to go off to his dad's, and he bounded off with Stephen, chatting about his day as happily as ever. She hoped he was going to be able to sleep all right that night, and she wouldn't have more issues with Stephen complaining. He hadn't even mentioned the letter from the solicitor when he'd come to pick him up, but still that niggle of worry wiggled around inside her.

What if he was going to take Ollie and refuse to bring him back again? What if he fed poisonous thoughts into Ollie's head about her—maybe even making him think she was replacing him with Haiden?

But she could only assume from Stephen's change in demeanour that the things she'd said to him on the phone about how impractical it would be for him to take Ollie during the week had actually got through his thick skull. She hoped he'd also accepted what she'd said about how unreliable Stephen was, and how there was nothing between her and Haiden and only had him staying because of the money. She doubted this momentary truce would last, however.

Even though it was Friday night, Haiden was sitting on the couch, watching *Gardener's World*. For someone who was only twenty-three, she got the impression he was far older at times. She paused in the doorway, her arms folded as she observed him engrossed in the programme, even though he'd never mentioned being particularly interested in gardening, with the exception of the pots he'd recreated for her.

"Don't you have friends at the university you should be out with on a Friday night?" she asked him.

He glanced away from the show and rewarded her with a smile, a dimple appearing in his left cheek. "Not really. It's a strange age bracket to be in. Everyone there seems to be either eighteen and having barely left home, or they're much older."

"Like me, you mean?" she said, only half teasing.

"Not at all. You're not older. I mean, these people are in their fifties and trying to fill in time created by an empty nest."

"Right." She suddenly felt sad at the idea of Haiden all alone and with no friends at the university. Maybe it was the maternal side of her. She couldn't help putting Ollie in everyone else's position.

"Anyway," Haiden said, "you're hardly one to talk. Don't you ever go out?"

"Out?" The question surprised her. "Well, I work, and take care of Ollie. We go to the park and the shops…"

She trailed off, realising she didn't have too much more to add.

He laughed. "I meant *out* out. Don't you ever go and do something fun?"

"I enjoy spending time with Ollie. That's fun to me." God, that sounded so lame.

"What about the weekends like this, where he's at his dads?"

She couldn't tell him that she was always too broke to do anything. That she didn't want to spend precious money on restaurants, or even cafes, or hairdressers and nail salons. It would just feel too selfish, too self-indulgent.

She shrugged. "Honestly, I enjoy the peace and quiet. I'm surrounded by kids all day at work, and then I come home and take care of Ollie. It's relaxing for me to take a bath and read a book, and just... you know, hang out."

She couldn't tell him how fearsomely lonely she found those weekends—how the hours stretched on forever, and she lay awake half the night, torturing herself that Ollie was also awake, upset and needing her.

He gave her that lopsided smile. "Except now you have me hanging around, too, so I guess I've ruined your peace and quiet."

She flapped a hand. "Oh, no, I didn't mean it like that. I'm happy to have you around. It's good to have some adult company, too."

"So, since your peace and quiet is already ruined, why not let me take you out tomorrow night? Doesn't need to be anything much—maybe the cinema? I don't know many people around here either. I'd appreciate the company."

"The cinema?"

"Yes, you know that place with the big screens that shows lots of different films?"

He was teasing her now, she could tell by the tone of his voice, and it only made her mortification grow. She couldn't go to the cinema with him, could she? It wasn't as though it was a date. They were just two people thrown together who were making good use of their free time.

She had to keep reminding herself that she wasn't in her twenties anymore. The way she saw him was completely different to how she saw her—and even if it wasn't, to even consider the possibility that this would go any further was utterly irresponsible. True, it wasn't as though he was underage or anything, but he was under her care, in a way.

She shook the thought from her head. It was ridiculous even thinking this way. It wasn't how Haiden was seeing this at all—she was just his frumpy landlady who already had tons of baggage. He was only offering this because he hadn't made any friends here yet.

"You know what," she said, "what the hell. Let's do it."

His face broke in a smile. "Yeah? That would be great. Anything you want to see?"

"As long as it's got plenty of action, I'm good." The last thing she wanted was to end up in a cinema with him watching a sexy romance, or a tear-jerker that was going to make her cry.

"Great, so it's a date."

"I'll look forward to it," she said, already hoping she wasn't getting herself into something she couldn't handle.

Chapter Fifteen

She did her best to avoid Haiden most of Saturday daytime, worried he'd notice how nervous she was at the prospect of going to the cinema with him that evening. She kept reminding herself how ridiculous she was being, and that they were only going to the cinema together as two adults who didn't have anyone else to go with. It didn't mean anything more than that. But she still wished she had Ollie around to distract her.

When the evening approached, she shut herself in her room and agonised over what she should wear and how much makeup she should apply. She wanted to make an effort, but not too much of an effort. In the end, she settled on a pair of her smarter jeans and a stripy top, and just applied a little mascara and lip gloss. Of course, Haiden didn't need to worry about things like makeup, and he'd be able to throw on any old thing and still look great.

A light knock came at her bedroom door. "You ready in there? We should probably get going if we're going to make the film."

"Just coming!" she chirped back, her heart racing.

Heat flushed her cheeks, and she sucked in a breath. This was just the cinema. It was no big deal.

She opened the door.

"Ready?" he asked, still waiting for her. Was it her imagination, or did his gaze drop down her body?

"Ready," she confirmed and brushed past his tall form to head down the stairs. She was going to drive, so she wouldn't be able to have a drink. She had the tolerance of a child and didn't trust herself under the influence of even one glass of wine.

Haiden had already pre-bought the tickets—his treat, he insisted.

She drove into town and found somewhere to park. They chatted easily about other films they'd both seen, and what had been their favourites and which ones they'd hated. Now that she was out of the house, she was finding it easier to relax, and she had to remind herself that this was something people did for enjoyment and not to torture themselves.

Their seats were in the middle row of the cinema, and she was relieved they weren't in the back row. Even though she knew she was overthinking everything, she was still hugely aware of the proximity of their bodies as they sat, side by side, waiting for the film to start. The heat of his shoulder burned into hers, and whenever he relaxed, his thigh bumped hers.

They'd treated themselves to popcorn, and a pick-n-mix for her, which Haiden kept delving into, despite him insisting he'd prefer popcorn and that the sweets were meant for children. They sat through the film, comfortable with each other, and for the next hour and a half, Kristen forgot she was his landlady, and older than he was, and that she had a son and a dickhead of an ex-husband to deal with.

When the film finished, they emerged onto the street. It was dark now, and town had filled up with young people in revealing, fashionable clothing, already slightly drunk, giggling and shouting to one another.

Kristen pulled her phone from her handbag, checking that Stephen hadn't called her about Ollie. To her dismay, she had five missed calls, but all of them were from Violet. Her stomach sank, but she shoved the phone into her bag, unable to deal with her sister right now. She was allowed to have one evening where she didn't have to constantly worry about other people.

"That was good, wasn't it?" she said to Haiden, half-wondering if he wished he was a part of all the young people walking past, enjoying themselves.

"Yeah, it was, but I enjoyed more than just the film.

She blinked up at him. "You did?"

He linked his fingers through hers, and her heart stopped.

"I really enjoy your company, Kristen. We haven't known each other long, but the first moment I set eyes on you, it was like something jumpstarted inside me."

"Haiden...."

"I'm not kidding. It was like an electric jolt."

How could she tell him that she'd felt the same way?

"And then," he continued, "I've got to know you, and this beautiful woman turns out to be pretty amazing, too. You're an incredible mother to Ollie, and I can see how you'll fight for him with every breath you have. You'll sacrifice everything for other people. You're stunning, and you have absolutely no idea. The younger women I meet are all so self-obsessed. They're more worried about making sure they get the perfect selfie or looking good on social media than doing anything meaningful in real life."

Her cheeks flushed hot. She could barely believe he was saying all this stuff to her. It had been so long since anyone had made her think she might be worth something that she almost didn't want to believe it. But what reason would he have to lie? If he was just interested in something physical, she was sure there were a hundred different apps that would help him hook up with some gorgeous twenty-year-old.

She opened her mouth to tell him that she didn't know what to say, but he leaned into her, and his lips pressed to hers. Involuntarily, her body melted against him, and her lips parted. His tongue softly brushed against hers, and she groaned, her arm snaking around his waist to pull him closer. He still had one of her hands in his, their fingers linked, and he lifted his other hand to thread it through her hair.

God, it had been so long since she'd been kissed like this—deep and passionate, and as though nothing else existed. The rest of the world fell away. They were standing outside of the cinema, making out like a couple of teenagers.

But they weren't teenagers. She was a divorced woman in her thirties with a son to think about. And this wasn't just some guy she'd met. He was a student she was supposed to be taking care of.

She broke the kiss and stepped back, even though a dull ache appeared in her chest at the lack of contact. "I'm sorry, Haiden. I just can't."

He frowned down at her. "Why not?"

She motioned between them. "This isn't how it's supposed to go. You're a student, and I'm supplying you with housing and meals. That's all."

"I'm a student, but I'm a mature student. I can understand if I was younger, but I'm not. We're both adults, and we should be allowed to make whatever choices we want."

She groaned and pushed both her hands through her hair. "It's not that simple. I'm sure it's not like we're doing anything illegal, but morally, it's a grey line."

An image of Nancy's face if she found out that Kristen had been making out with one of their students flashed into her mind, and she shrivelled inside.

"Really?" He sounded disbelieving.

"Haiden, you're the first student I've taken in, and I really can't afford to mess this up. If the university finds out, I might be struck off the register, and once you leave, they won't place any more students with me."

He took a step closer, a tweak of a smile on his perfect lips. "I could always not leave," he said, his voice husky.

She placed a hand to his chest to prevent him coming any closer. "Don't even joke about it."

Despite everything that had been going on lately, she had to admit she'd been happier with Haiden around. She'd missed adult company, and his company was especially enjoyable.

"But seriously," she continued, "I just can't take the risk. I really need the money—not only for me, but for Ollie, too. I can't have this all blowing up in my face."

"Hey, that's okay. I understand."

"Thank you. I can hardly believe I turned you down. I mean, look at you." She gestured helplessly towards him. She must be mad.

"You should look at yourself a little more closely, too, Kristen," he said softly. "And I don't mean that in a bad way. I honestly don't think you see yourself the way the rest of the world does."

She gave him a rueful smile. "That's kind of you to say."

"You should believe it."

"I'm trying," she lied. She glanced over her shoulder in the direction of where she'd parked the car. "I guess we should probably be getting home."

It was still early, but she didn't want to feel awkward, just the two of them after that kiss. She wanted to shut herself away in her room and over think everything for a few hours until she eventually fell asleep.

Chapter Sixteen

The next morning, she woke to the sound of voices coming from downstairs.

Kristen sat up in bed, frowning. Had Stephen brought Ollie home already? She checked the time and winced. It was gone ten in the morning. Far later than she normally slept in. But then she'd not managed to sleep until about two, her thoughts turning over and over and refusing to let her rest. She hadn't been able to stop thinking about Haiden. She'd even wondered if it was possible for Haiden to request a move to a different accommodation, but then she'd shut that idea down. He'd have to give a reason for wanting to move, and whatever excuse they came up with, it was always going to reflect badly on her. Besides, even if he moved to a different location and they carried on seeing each other, he would have to go back to Sweden in a couple of months. There was no positive outcome in all of this. It was no surprise she had slept so late.

But no, one of the voices was definitely female.

What the hell was going on?

She slipped out of bed and pulled on her dressing gown. There was only one person she knew who would turn up at her house unannounced.

Kristen padded downstairs, following the voices into the living room. As she got closer, she realised the person sounded upset and her stomach twisted. Not that her being upset was anything unusual, but Kristen didn't normally wake up to find her already in her house.

The living room door was partially shut, so she pushed it open and stepped through.

Violet was sitting on their sofa, her head in her hands. Haiden sat beside her, his arm around her shoulders, which shuddered beneath his touch. Both looked up as she stepped in, and though Violet's eyes were rimmed with red, Kristen couldn't see any actual tears.

She didn't miss how closely she was snuggled up to Haiden, however, and anger burned through her. What the hell was Violet playing at now? She warned her sister to stay away from Haiden, and here she was with his arm around her. Maybe Kristen was a little jealous after the kiss she'd shared with Haiden, but mostly she was angry because no matter what she told Violet, no matter how important all this was, when Violet wanted something, she just strode in a took it.

Haiden looked up at her with an anxious smile. "Oh, Kristen. Good morning."

She didn't reply but focused her attention on her sister. "What are you doing here, Violet?"

Violet sniffed and rubbed her eyes. "I needed to see my sister, is that all right? I called you last night, but you never answered."

"It doesn't look like you wanted to see me," she said, her tone sharp.

"Haiden said you were still sleeping. We didn't want to wake you."

We. That stung.

Kristen jammed her hands on her hips, aware Violet hadn't answered the question. "What are you doing here?" she repeated.

Violet covered her mouth with her fingers, her eyes casting down, her shoulders shaking. God, she was a good actress when she wanted to be. "I had a panic attack this morning. I thought I was going to die."

"Right. But you didn't. You're fine."

"I don't know how you can be so calm about everything all the time, Kristen. You went through exactly the same as me, and yet you always seem to hold everything together."

Her blood ran cold. She didn't want Haiden knowing about what their childhood had been like. It wasn't any of his business, and truthfully, she didn't want him to think any differently of her.

"This isn't the time to talk about it."

"It never is the time, though, it is, Kristen?" she continued. "You just want to pretend like we didn't grow up with a completely crazy mother."

"Stop it, Violet," she warned.

Haiden was looking between them, curiosity sparking in his blue eyes.

Violet turned to him. "Our mother was batshit," she told him. "She wasn't too bad when we were little—or perhaps we didn't know any different—but then as soon as Kristen hit puberty, she kind of lost it. She couldn't stand to see us growing up and wanted to keep us as little girls."

"She was frightened for us," Kristen murmured, feeling awkward, uncomfortable. She didn't want to go through this again and didn't want Haiden to know about it. But short of throwing herself at her sister and clamping her hand over her mouth, which would look even worse, there wasn't much she could do.

"Kristen protected me from the worst of her madness," Violet said, "but it wasn't easy. We were horribly picked on at school because we were never allowed the things other teenagers had. Other kids had cool stuff, while we were only allowed dolls, and tea-sets, and we weren't allowed out. Then eventually she yanked us out of regular school and home-schooled us, which made us even more isolated."

"Haiden doesn't need to know all of this," Kristen interrupted.

He glanced up at her. "It's fine, really. I want to know."

But maybe I don't want you to know, she thought but didn't say.

"She wouldn't accept it when we got our periods, and poor Kristen had to go and steal sanitary products."

She blushed at the memory. "Okay, that's enough now."

But Violet hadn't finished. "I often wonder how Kristen's going to be when Ollie gets older." She turned her attention to her sister. "Do you think there's much of Mum in you, Kristen? Do you think you'll struggle when Ollie starts to get independent, too?"

She looked at her, baffled. "What? No, of course not."

"You can get a bit obsessive about things like she did. The money pinching and stuff like that."

Her mouth dropped open. "I'm nothing like Mum was!"

"Really? 'Cause I remember all those little sayings she had..."

"Shut the hell up, Violet! How dare you come into my house and start throwing all this shit at me?"

She no longer cared that Haiden was sitting right there.

Violet jumped to her feet. "I came because I'd had a panic attack, and I was hoping for a little sympathy from my big sister. But I should have known I wouldn't be able to count on that. You say you're nothing like Mum, but she never saw what was going on outside of her own head either."

"Get out, Violet. I don't need this shit first thing in the morning."

"Can't cope with it, huh? Jeez, lucky Ollie isn't here. Maybe the boy is better off with his dad."

Kristen grabbed Violet by the arm and marched her towards the front door.

She shook her off. "I can go. You don't need to manhandle me."

Kristen yanked open the front door. "Go, then."

"Fine, I will. See, I told you that you were crazy."

She tossed her hair over one shoulder and marched down the garden path, violently slamming the gate shut as she went.

Kristen let out a growl of frustration and slammed the front door shut as well. Tears of frustration welled in her eyes. How did Violet always manage to have this effect on her? Why couldn't the two of them just get on? They had, when they were younger. Violet had been right when she'd said that Kristen had taken the worst of their mother's erratic behaviour. She remembered how much she'd loved Violet—taking care of her little sister had been the most important thing in her life. But now it felt like everything she did or said was wrong, and the only thing Violet cared about was herself.

Movement at the living room door caught her attention and she looked to find Haiden half propped against the doorframe, watching her in concern.

"Are you okay? I'm sorry I let her in without checking with you first."

She swiped her eyes with the back of her hand. "No, it's not your fault. That's just what my relationship with Violet is like. We seem incapable of not pushing each other's buttons."

"Was what she said about your mother true?"

"Yes, it was," she admitted.

He nodded sympathetically. "I know what it's like to grow up in a bad household."

She looked up at him in surprise. "I thought you were close to your family."

"Oh, well, I am now." He glanced down and scuffed his foot across the carpet. "We had some issues when I was younger, though. My dad had some problems with drink, but he's got it under control now. He's not touched a drop in years."

"Oh, right. I'm sorry to hear that."

Was that why Haiden hadn't been in touch with his family? She wanted to mention it, but she already understood how difficult it was talking about dark family matters, and she didn't want to put him in the same position.

Haiden shrugged. "That's okay. It's in the past now, right?"

"Right," she agreed.

A smile widened across his handsome face. "Better to focus on the future."

Chapter Seventeen

"Hurry up, Ollie. We should have left five minutes ago!" Ollie appeared at the top of the stairs, his hair still flattened on one side where he'd slept on it.

Stephen had dropped him off the previous day, with still no mention of the solicitor's letter. She hoped that was the end of the subject, and while she desperately wanted to know what Stephen had planned, she didn't want to be the one to bring it up and reignite the conversation if there was no need.

Ollie flew down the stairs towards her, and she caught him long enough to restyle his hair with her fingers. "You'll have to do," she said, mainly to herself.

Haiden had left for the bus half an hour ago. Neither of them had mentioned either the kiss they'd shared on the Saturday night, or Violet's revelations about their upbringing yesterday. She appreciated him being discreet, but a part of her longed for him to mention the kiss. It was the first time she'd kissed a man since her divorce, and she couldn't pretend like it didn't mean anything to her. She was still in disbelief someone like Haiden even felt that way about someone like her, but no one had forced him to say those lovely things about her or kiss her in that way.

Kristen grazed the tips of her fingers to her lips, relishing the memory of how the kiss had felt for just a moment longer before she had to let the rest of the world in.

"Muuum," a little voice whined from beside her. "You said we were going to be late."

"Yes, of course," she said, snapping herself from her reverie. "Let's go."

She snatched up her bag and the items Ollie needed for school before stepping out of the front door and locking it behind her. They walked down the garden path together and stepped out onto the pavement.

Her car was parked a little way along the street outside—they had no allocated parking and just had to hope they'd get somewhere close to the house—and they had to walk past it on their way up to school. The car seemed to be on a lean, and she frowned as they got closer.

Her mouth dropped open. "What the hell?"

From the side she was standing on, on the pavement, she could see that both of her tyres were flat.

"Wait there," she told Ollie, positioning him away from the road.

"What's wrong?"

"Nothing. Just stay put for a minute, okay?"

She dropped his hand, checked for traffic, and then stepped out into the road to round the vehicle. To her dismay, the other two tyres were the same.

"Shit, shit, shit!"

"Mummy! You said a bad word," Ollie scolded her. "You said it three times!"

"Sorry, sweetie."

She exhaled a long sigh and went back onto the pavement to join him. Thank God they could just walk to school and she wasn't going to need the car to get into work, but she still needed use of the car to go food shopping or head into town. How much was this going to cost her? New tyres were expensive, and she had no idea if this sort of thing was covered under her insurance. What the hell had happened, anyway? Had she driven over some glass?

"Come on, let's get you to breakfast club. We're already late."

There was nothing she could do about the car right now. She needed to get to work, and she knew she was already in the headteacher's bad books for kicking up a fuss about Felix Hurst. In fact, she'd never figured out if he'd even had the chat with the two boys that he'd promised.

She glanced down at Ollie, half-skipping happily along beside her. He was in a good mood, and she didn't want to spoil things by bringing up the bullying, or that he was supposed to have had a little talk with the headteacher. She knew each of those things would upset him, and she had enough on her mind without having to worry about getting Ollie into breakfast club when he was upset about something. Maybe it wasn't her finest parenting moment, but sometimes she just needed to do what she could to get through.

After dropping Ollie off, she called the local garage and told them what had happened. The car would need to be brought in for that many tyres to be replaced and they could send the tow truck that afternoon. Thank goodness for the extra money Haiden's board had brought in. Though she never would have wanted to spend the money on the car, at least she had it.

She went straight to the headteacher's office. Andrew Larson was in his usual position behind his desk, and he looked up when she knocked and popped her head around the door.

"Andrew, I'm really sorry to do this, but is there any chance I can take an hour off this afternoon? I've had a bit of an emergency I need to deal with."

He frowned at her, and her heart sank. "Really, Kristen? Can't it be done at another time?"

"I'll take it as my lunch break," she insisted. "It's just the tow truck is coming for my car and I don't have any way of getting to the garage, so I'm hoping they'll give me a lift. I'll try to get back as soon as I can."

He exhaled another long sigh but waved her away. "Fine, but if any extra work builds up, you'll have to stay late to do it."

"Not a problem. Thanks, Andrew."

For once, it would be nice of him to be on her side, to just say 'sure, Kristen. Take the day off if you need it.' She was a good employee and couldn't even remember the last time she'd had a day off sick, but he treated her like she was nothing more than a constant inconvenience.

With a sigh, and wishing she could catch a break just once, she went to her own office and sat down. She needed to stay ahead of things if she wasn't going to be here until seven that night.

"I'M GOING TO HEAD OFF now, Anna," she announced after working through her lunch break. She grabbed her handbag out from under the desk. "You going to be okay without me?"

"I'm sure I'll be fine. Hope they can fix your car."

"Thanks. Hope I can afford for them to fix my car."

She left the school and hurried home, conscious of the time. As she approached her street, the tow truck was already there.

"Hi," she said, hurrying up to the two men who looked like they were dealing with things. "I'm the owner. Kristen Scott."

The bigger of the two men turned towards her. "Oh, hi. This is your car?"

"Yes, it is. I came out this morning and found it like this."

"Have you called the police and reported it?"

She jolted back in shock. "What? No, why would I?"

His big, meaty slab of a forehead crumpled in a frown. "I'm sorry, but it looks like someone's done this on purpose."

"What do you mean?"

"I mean you've got great big slashes in each of your tyres. Looks like someone's taken a kitchen knife to them to me."

She ran cold. "Couldn't I have just run over something? I drove the car to the supermarket yesterday afternoon. Maybe I did it then."

She didn't like the thought that someone else had done this to her vehicle. Was it just a couple of kids out causing trouble, or was this more menacing and someone had attacked her car on purpose?

"Unless you ran over someone holding a couple of large knives, I'd say that was pretty unlikely."

"Shit."

She ran her hand through her hair and shook her head in disbelief. Someone had done this deliberately. But who? The memory of her fight with Violet popped into her head. Surely Violet wouldn't have done this to her car, no matter how angry she was. Violet could be a little unstable at times, but she knew how short of money Kristen was, and that this would cost a fortune to repair. No matter how bad things were between them, Violet had never resorted to destroying her property.

She thought back to the broken flowerpots. Or maybe Violet *had* destroyed her property before, and it was just that she'd never linked the two.

She let out a sigh. "Okay, thanks. Do you need me to come to the garage now?"

"Nah, we'll give you a call when we get everything priced up."

"If there's any way of doing this the cheapest way possible, I'd really appreciate it."

"There's no way we can mend the tyres, but we might have some second-hand ones we can source for you. That'll keep the price down."

"Thanks. I'd really appreciate it. Things are a little tight at the moment."

He gave her a rueful smile. "I know the feeling."

It was a small kindness, but it brought tears to her eyes.

She left them to go back to school. He'd said she should report this to the police, but if Violet was responsible, did she really want to get the cops involved?

Chapter Eighteen

"How did it go?" Anna asked when she got back to school. "All sorted?"

"As much as it can be, for now."

She considered confiding in Anna about what the tow truck guy had said, but then decided not to. Anna liked to gossip, and she didn't want it getting around that someone had slashed her tyres deliberately. A chill ran through her at the thought. What if it wasn't Violet, and was someone else she hadn't even thought of? She liked to think she didn't have many enemies, but that wasn't exactly the truth, was it? Lately, it felt like she had more enemies than friends.

The bell rang to signal the end of school. While she wasn't finished with her work yet, she knew the afterschool club Ollie attended allowed the children to have a play for fifteen minutes or so to burn off some steam. She caught his eye through the window and gave him a wave before he ran off again.

The phone rang, and she answered it. One of the parents was running late, and they'd need their child watched until they could get there—ten or fifteen minutes at the most.

Shouts came from the playground.

Her heart thumped, and she jumped to her feet. Instinctively, she knew it had to do with Ollie. Kristen ran out of the office and into the playground. Though school was over, some of the kids had been having a run around before going home, the mums standing in small groups and catching up on the gossip.

Ollie should have been with the afterschool club group, who were given a separate area of the playground, but instead she saw him tussling with Felix, a small gang of other boys standing around them.

"Hey!" she yelled. "Hey, stop that, now!"

She ran over and grabbed both boys, pulling them apart. She was shocked to see blood running from Ollie's nose, while the bigger boy looked fine except for ruffled hair and his shirt pulled out of his trousers.

"What the hell is going on here?" she demanded.

Both boys stared sullenly at the ground, refusing to answer.

"Are you okay, baby?" she asked her son, fishing into her pocket for a tissue and giving it to him to put to his bleeding nose.

The clip-clop of high heels marched towards them.

She turned to discover Rachelle standing behind her, immaculately dressed as always, an expression of concern on her made-up face.

"Felix was fighting with Ollie again," Kristen snapped.

"He started it," Felix said, sulkily.

Kristen let out a huff of air. "Oh, please. How did Ollie start it?"

Felix poked out his lower lip. "He called me a name. I heard him!"

Ollie looked both baffled and worried. "No, I didn't. I was just playing, and he told me to come over 'cause he wanted to ask me something."

Rachelle stepped in. "Then we just have two children's words against each other."

Kristen ignored her and looked to Felix. "Is that true?"

"No! He called me an idiot. I heard him!"

"Even if Ollie did call you an idiot," she said, "which I highly doubt he did, that's no reason to punch him in the nose."

"I didn't. He must have hit it on the ground or something."

"See," Rachelle said, "Felix didn't even hit him. It was just an accident."

Kristen saw red. She'd had enough of this woman making out like her son was innocent all the time, when that clearly wasn't the case. Before she had even considered what she was doing, she spun around to face Rachelle.

"I swear to God," she said, shoving a finger into Rachelle's smug face, "if you won't punish your kid for hurting mine, I'll do it myself."

Her eyes widened, her mouth dropping open in aghast horror. "Did you just threaten my son?"

"I mean it, Rachelle. If Felix lays a single finger on Ollie again, I'll show him exactly how it feels to be bitten, and hit, and pushed over." Her fury was blinding, the words pouring from her mouth. She was so angry and frustrated—frustrated at the school's insistence they'd done everything they could to protect Ollie, when that clearly wasn't the case, and frustrated by Rachelle's refusal to see and accept what a horrible little bully her son was. Kristen had never hurt a child, and had no intention of doing so, but she just wanted this all to stop. She'd worked hard for so many years to hold everything together, that to have it all fall apart because of one six-year-old boy felt horrendously unfair.

"You can't go around physically threatening small children," Rachelle snapped. "What the hell is wrong with you? You work at a school, and you think that kind of behaviour is all right? I'm afraid that if you plan to hurt my child, how many other children are you thinking about hurting."

Kristen stuttered, jerking back in shock. "What? No, that's not what I'm saying at all. I don't plan on hurting children!"

"Really? Because that's not what it sounded like to me. Frankly, Kristen, I think this has become a safe-guarding issue now, and really needs to be reported."

She spluttered with disbelief. "You have got to be kidding me! Your son is violent towards mine, day after day, and you think *I'm* the one who is the safe-guarding issue?"

"The boys are just children. They rough and tumble a little. It's perfectly normal, and perhaps it will help Ollie to toughen up instead of being so overprotected all the time."

Kristen clenched her fists to her sides to prevent herself launching at the other woman and clawing her face off. She'd never been a violent person, but somehow the combination of Rachelle and Felix sparked something inside her. All she was trying to do was take care of her child—that was all she'd ever wanted to do—and now somehow that was demonising her.

Just like her mother.

"Stop making excuses for Felix," she managed to splutter. "It's not play if one of the children involved doesn't want to be and ends up getting hurt. I won't put up with it anymore, Rachelle!"

Her eyes were hard and cold. "Yeah, I heard you. You'll hurt Felix, isn't that what you said?"

"Stop twisting my words and think about parenting your son properly instead."

Not letting her get another word in, she took Ollie by the hand and marched him towards the bathrooms. She needed to clean up his poor nose and then she'd take him home early. Screw whatever Andrew might think about it. Taking care of Ollie was more important than trying to please a headteacher who was consistently failing him.

BACK AT HOME, SHE PREPARED dinner, close to tears the entire time. She kept replaying what had been said in the playground, wishing she'd handled things differently. She should have kept her temper, she knew that now, but that, combined with the slashed car tyres, and her sister, and Stephen, had all just been too much, and she'd snapped.

Kristen bent to take the tray containing the jacket potatoes out of the oven. Grabbing the edges in a tea towel, she slid the tray out.

"Shit!"

It had been hotter and heavier than she'd anticipated, and the tray slipped from her fingers, spilling cooked potatoes all over the floor.

Kristen stared down at their ruined dinner and burst into tears.

"Hey." A concerned male voice came from behind her. "What's wrong?"

Firm hands on her shoulders pulled her around, and she found her face pressed to a broad chest. Haiden's comforting scent surrounded her, and he wrapped his arms around her shoulders, holding her tight. The heat of his breath warmed the top of her head as she cried against his shirt.

"I'm sorry," she said, embarrassed by her tears. "It's just been a really horrible day."

He released her and quickly stooped to pick up the potatoes. "Three second rule?"

She gave a wane smile. "More like three-minute rule."

"It'll be fine. We just won't eat the skin."

"Thanks Haiden." She swiped her tears away with her palm.

"You want to tell me what happened?" he asked, setting the potatoes back down on the tray.

She considered not telling him, but realised she'd feel better by sharing. There wasn't anything he could do about it, but a problem shared, and all that. She filled him in on everything, from the slashed tyres to the issues at school. Haiden listened, his normally smooth brow furrowed.

"That's horrible," he said when she'd finished. "No wonder you're upset."

"It'll be fine. I've been through worse than this and come out of it. You just caught me at a bad time. I'm sorry I unloaded on you. This isn't your problem."

He reached out and touched her chin, so she lifted her face to his, her heart thumping for a whole different reason. "You can unload on me anytime, Kristen. I'm right here for you, okay?"

For the first time that day, she smiled. "Okay."

It felt good to have someone on her side, for once.

Chapter Nineteen

The next day she dropped Ollie off at breakfast club as usual and went into her office. Her backside had barely hit her chair when Andrew appeared in the doorway.

"Kristen, can I speak with you for a moment, please?"

She shot straight back out of her chair and exchanged a glance with Anna, who was already at her desk on the other side of the room. "Oh, sure. Of course."

She followed him out and into his office. It was still early, so the other children and parents hadn't shown up yet, and the school was quiet, but she was surprised to see Margaret Dean sitting in the office as well.

"Good morning, Margaret," she said to the head of the school Governors.

Margaret gave her a tight smile but didn't say good morning in return.

"Please, sit," Andrew said, gesturing to a chair on the other side of his desk.

Unease twisted like a whirlpool inside her.

"I'm afraid I've had a complaint from one of the other parents that you threatened to hurt their child. I'm sure you understand that this is a serious matter, which is why I've had to bring Margaret in to oversee this meeting"

Her mouth dropped open. "By one of the *other parents,* you mean Rachelle Hurst?"

"I'm afraid I can't disclose who made the complaint."

She clenched her teeth. "That's okay. You don't need to."

"So, you admit the conversation happened? That you threatened to hurt the boy?"

"I was angry and frustrated. He's been picking on Ollie constantly—physically hurting him—as you know. I've come to you about this several times now, and nothing changes. You haven't made any attempt to discipline him, when the kid should have been suspended by now for what he's put Ollie through."

"Kristen, when I've spoken to the boys before, Ollie says they're playing, and things just get a little rough."

She snorted. "Yeah, right. What else is he going to say when you have the other boy sitting right there? Ollie is terrified of him. He's not going to tell tales."

"But I think you're missing the point, Kristen. You can't go around threatening the children, especially not when you work here. The most important part of our jobs is making sure the children are safe during their time here."

"Ollie hasn't been safe!" she blurted.

He lifted a hand to silence her. "I'm afraid I'm going to have to suspend you, effective immediately, while we look into matters further."

"You have got to be kidding me." Her mind pulled in at the edges, and she gripped the armrests of the chair, suddenly feeling like this was all a bad dream and she wasn't quite there anymore.

"Frankly, I've been a little concerned about your performance at work lately. You've taken time off, and I've found you sneaking off to make personal phone calls during work time, which you know isn't allowed."

She could hardly believe it. This was so unfair. "I've had some family emergencies I've had to deal with. But tell me, Mr. Larsen, is this suspension about my work performance, or what I said to Rachelle, because it can't be both."

"It's the threat, Kristen. I just thought I'd mention the other concerns so you can give them some consideration during your suspension."

She clamped her jaw together, resisting the urge to tell him to fuck off. She needed this job, and she'd grovel to get it back, if she had to, even though every time she saw Rachelle in the playground or at school meetings, she was going to want to claw the other woman's eyes out. That bitch. That *fucking* bitch.

She got to her feet, her legs wobbling beneath her. Her stomach felt weak and her hands were shaking. Her thoughts immediately went to Ollie. She was going to have to go and see him before school started. He'd want to know why she wasn't in the office as normal. With everything else going on, it just seemed wrong that he was going to have this thrown at him as well.

A couple of steps took her towards the office door, but then she stopped and turned around.

"You know, I wouldn't have needed to resort to this if you'd just dealt with Felix Hurst properly."

She didn't let him reply, knowing she was horribly close to tears and not wanting either of them to see them. Yanking open the door, she put her head down and went back to her own office. She needed to collect her coat and bag, and let Anna know she'd be working on her own today. Who would they bring in to cover her while she wasn't there? There was no way Anna could handle everything by herself. It was hard enough when one of them had a day off, never mind a suspension. If he brought in Rachelle to cover her job, she thought she might scream.

Anna looked up with concerned curiosity as she walked in. Kristen went straight to her desk, swiping any personal items into her handbag.

"What's wrong? What happened?"

"I've been suspended."

"What? Why?"

"I threatened Rachelle that I'd hurt Felix if she didn't do something to stop him bullying Ollie. Apparently, that's a safe-guarding issue now that needs to be looked into."

"I can't believe Rachelle ratted you out. What a bitch!"

Kristen shook her head, her anger deflating to sadness and regret. "It's my own fault. I never should have said it. I was just so angry. Now I have to go and tell Ollie that Mummy won't be at school for the foreseeable future. With everything else going on, I really don't know how he's going to take it."

Anna rose from her desk and put her arms around Kristen and hugged her tight. "Oh, honey. I'm so sorry."

The tears threatened again, and she waved at her face and blinked quickly to hold them back. "It's okay. Don't be nice to me. You'll make me cry."

"Okay." She gave her a sympathetic smile. "But call me if you need me, okay? I can always drop Ollie home to you if you feel you can't face coming up here."

"At least he won't need to go to breakfast or afterschool club," she said, trying to think of the silver lining. Damn, she needed this job, though. What was she going to do if she got fired? She didn't have any savings, and she still needed to pay the mortgage. Thank God for Haiden and the hosting money. If she didn't have that coming in, she'd be beside herself right now. Shit, she already was beside herself. She loved her job. She prided herself in working for a living, and still being there for Ollie. This wasn't how she'd intended for things to go at all.

With a heavy heart, she picked up the rest of her things and left the office. She crossed the playground to where the building for the breakfast club was located.

One of the women who worked there looked over at her, a question in her eyes.

"I just need to speak to Ollie a minute," she said.

The woman nodded. "Of course. Ollie, your mummy's here to see you."

Ollie dropped what he was doing and ran over to her, slamming into her legs in a hug, as though he hadn't seen her for days, not the fifteen minutes since she'd dropped him off. She hugged him back and then dropped to a crouch, so their faces were level.

"Ollie, I'm not going to be in the office for a while. Something has happened, and I need to go home. I just wanted you to know so you didn't get a surprise when you saw I wasn't there."

His little forehead wrinkled in a frown. "Why won't you be there?"

She wasn't sure how much to tell him. "I said something I shouldn't have, and now I'm in a bit of trouble for it."

His chin trembled. "So, you're like... in time out?"

She forced a smile. "Yeah, something like that. Time out for grownups. Hey, but the good news is that it means you won't have to come to breakfast club or afterschool club until this all gets sorted out. So, I'll be here to pick you up at the end of school like the other mums."

A smile spread across his face. "I get to go home straight after school?"

"Yep."

"Cool." He threw his arms around her neck and hugged her again, and then spun back around and ran back to where he was playing with a car garage set.

Kristen got to her feet and made her way over to where the woman who ran the breakfast and afterschool club was filling in some forms, a cup of coffee on the table next to her.

"I don't know if you overheard, but Ollie won't be coming to breakfast and afterschool club for the next couple of weeks."

"Right. Do you want me to keep his spot open for him? I will have to still charge you for the time, though, even if he's not here. It's a place another child could have."

With so many parents both needing to work these days just to pay the bills, the club was an invaluable resource. She didn't want to give up the spot, but she also couldn't afford to keep paying for something she didn't need.

"No, that's okay. You don't need to keep it open. I'll figure something out."

Her stomach sank, unsure if she was making the right choice. If she was allowed back into her role, she might struggle for childcare if she'd given her place away. But if she kept the place, she'd be spending money she would end up desperately needing if she didn't have a job.

She'd just have to take her chances, and hope something could be arranged when this all got sorted.

Chapter Twenty

It felt strange leaving the school to go home before it was even nine in the morning. Parents were starting to arrive with their children, and she sensed them giving her curious glances as they spotted her leaving early with her bag slung over her shoulder and her head down. She prayed none of them would stop to ask her any questions. Humiliation and shame washed over her, and she was worried she'd cry if anyone was even the slightest bit kind to her.

She was alert for any sign of Rachelle Hurst and Felix, too. She hated that she wasn't going to be in school to keep an eye on things. What if the bullying got worse, and Ollie didn't have the confidence to tell her?

Maybe she should consider pulling him out of school. If she wasn't going to be working there, perhaps it would be for the best. He did have friends, but he was only five and he'd make more somewhere else quickly enough. The school was convenient for where they lived, and she'd enjoyed him being at the school, up to this point. But now it felt like she'd been blacklisted, and that was only going to affect Ollie. Besides, it was clear nothing was going to be done about Felix, and she couldn't deal with him and Rachelle for the next five years.

It felt like running away, but maybe it was the right decision for them both.

Her phone buzzed, and she fished it out of her handbag. She glanced down at it and sighed. Violet's name appeared across the cracked screen. Kristen ignored the call and dropped the phone back into her bag. Her sister had been calling and sending numerous text messages telling her to stop ignoring her, but she couldn't bring herself to talk to her. The image of her car's slashed tyres was fresh in her mind—and she hadn't even managed to get the car back yet. Was Violet responsible? She didn't want to think so, but she knew if she was to see Violet, she'd have to ask her directly. Violet was bound to deny it, no matter if she was innocent or guilty, and would get defensive and they'd most likely fight again. With everything else going on, she just didn't feel like she had the emotional strength to deal with her sister right now.

She reached her house and placed the key in the lock. It felt strange to come home to an empty house and have the whole day during the week stretching ahead of her with nothing to do. She couldn't remember the last time that happened. Normally, she'd either be working, or Ollie would be home with her. Of course, she had the weekends when he was at his dad's, but somehow that felt different. At least at the weekend you were supposed to be off work. Right now, it felt like she was doing something she shouldn't by being here.

She turned the lock in the door and pushed it open. The postman had already been, and she stooped to pick up the letters waiting for her. She dumped them, unopened, on the hallway table. If one of them happened to contain anything close to bad news, she didn't think she'd be able to handle it. What she needed right now was a hot cup of tea and some time to process what had happened. She was shaken by the whole thing and wished more than anything that she hadn't confronted Rachelle. What could she do, though? She couldn't have allowed Felix to get away with hurting Ollie.

Movement came from upstairs, and she froze, her heart pounding, her stomach lurching.

Someone was up there.

She'd waved Haiden off to the bus that morning, and she'd just left Ollie at school—not that she'd have ever expected Ollie to be in the house alone anyway.

Shit.

Her phone was in her handbag. Had whoever was up there heard her come in? She should call the police and tell them she had an intruder in her home. No, she was over-reacting. It was most likely only Lemmy. He'd probably brought in a mouse or something and had taken it upstairs. Knowing him, he'd let it go and it had run under one of the beds or wardrobes, and the noise she'd heard was him trying to fish it back out again.

Despite her reassurances, her blood fizzed through her veins, her ears straining, all the hairs on her arms and the back of her neck standing to attention. Her heart pounded fast, stealing her breath.

Still clutching her handbag to her shoulder and not bothering to take off her shoes, she crept up the stairs. Before she reached the top, she stopped.

Lemmy was sound asleep on the landing, right under the radiator. He didn't look as though he'd done any mouse chasing recently.

Her pulse stepped up a notch, and she hesitated, wondering what to do. She hadn't heard anything else. Could she have imagined it?

There was no way she could just turn around and go back down the stairs and pretend she hadn't heard anything. She needed to check the bedrooms and make sure everything was as she'd left it.

Sucking in another shaky breath, her legs wobbly, she forced herself to take the remaining stairs. Lemmy heard her approach and opened one eye to acknowledge her. Surely if there was a stranger in the house, Lemmy would have made himself scarce.

Someone stepped out of her bedroom, and Kristen screamed, her hand clutched to her chest.

"Jesus Christ, Haiden. You just about gave me a heart attack. What are you doing here? I thought you'd got the bus to go to school."

"I forgot something," he said, sheepishly, holding up a folder. "I'm going to need to catch the next one." He must have realised something, as he frowned. "What are you doing home? I thought you would be at work."

She sighed heavily, relieved she wasn't going to have to fight off an intruder. "You know I told you about this bully Ollie has at school, and that I had a bit of an altercation with the mother the other day? Well, the headmaster sent me home."

"He sent you home because your son is being bullied?"

"No, he sent me home because of the fight I had with the other mother."

He lifted his eyebrows. "You had a fight with one of the other mothers?"

"Not like an actual fight," she said, amused at his shocked expression. "Just words were said that shouldn't have been, and it got me in trouble."

"I'm sorry to hear that. Poor Ollie. How's he doing?"

"He's okay, but I feel bad that I'm not there to watch out for him anymore. Not that it's been making any difference." She rubbed her hand over her eyes, suddenly exhausted. "If anything, I've only made things worse."

"Hey." He reached out and touched her upper arm, the contact and heat of his skin against hers making her jump, her heart racing for a different reason. "Ollie is lucky to have a mother who stands up for him. A lot of kids don't have that."

She gave him a smile, wishing in equal measures that he'd both remove his hand and also never let go.

"Anyway," he said, dropping his hand, "I'd better get going. I'm already late."

She nodded and stepped to one side to let him by. "Yes, of course."

He brushed past her, and it wasn't until he'd made it down the stairs and had left through the front door that she even question what he was doing in her room.

THE DAY PASSED BY PAINFULLY slowly.

She caught up on all her housework, and then started on some jobs she'd been putting off for ages—cleaning out the fridge and sorting out the cupboard under the sink. She couldn't bring herself to sit on the sofa and watch daytime television. Even the thought depressed her. She was tempted to pick up a book and take a long bath, but guilt kept her cleaning.

When three o'clock finally rolled around, she ached from the physical toil. Her stomach churned, knowing she was going to have to go back up to school and face everyone. She was ashamed of her suspension, and knew everyone would be gossiping and asking questions, wanting to know what had happened. Of course, Rachelle would be more than happy to tell everyone her version of events. People were probably claiming she'd held a knife to Felix's throat by this point.

Keeping her head down, not making eye contact with anyone, she hurried up to school. Ollie was waiting for her in the classroom, and she grabbed his stuff and got back out of there as quickly as possible.

Even on the walk home, she deliberately avoided stopping to talk to anyone.

Haiden wasn't back when she got home, and she forced herself to look at the bright side of things for Ollie's sake.

"You know," she told him as she placed a plate of chopped fruit in front of him at the kitchen table, "I always wanted to be able to do this when I was working."

"Do what?" Ollie looked up at her.

"Give you snacks straight after school instead of you having to go to afterschool club."

His expression dropped. "I did like playing with my friends, though."

She twisted her lips, that knot of anxiety tightening inside her. "Yeah, sorry, kiddo."

He finished his snack and jumped up from the table. "That's okay, Mummy. I'm going to go and play with my cars now."

"Sure, you do that."

Ollie disappeared into the other room, and she got to work starting dinner. It was earlier than they normally ate, but she figured there was no point in waiting.

The door slammed, signalling Haiden arriving home. She expected him to pop his head around the door, but instead heavy feet hurried up the stairs. Her stomach sank further. Having Haiden around made her feel better. But then she remembered how she'd come home earlier and found him in the house. He had every right to be here, but it had been strange how she'd caught him coming out of her bedroom. She needed to ask him about that. She was sure there was some innocent explanation, but she wanted to hear him say it.

When the food was ready, she called up the stairs for Haiden, and then stuck her head into the living room to get Ollie to the table as well.

"Something smells good," Haiden said as he entered the room.

She placed his plate on the table. "It's only shepherd's pie."

Now she was facing the prospect of being unemployed, she felt the reality of poverty weighing back down on her shoulders. She was going to have to start watching what kinds of foods they ate again.

"How was your day in the end?" she asked Haiden as she took a seat. "You didn't forget anything else?"

He frowned at her, his fork held halfway to his mouth. "Forget anything?"

"Yes, you were in my room earlier, remember?"

"Oh, yeah. Sorry about that. I was missing a t-shirt. I thought it might have got mixed up in the wash."

He'd been going through her drawers. That felt invasive. "You went through my stuff?"

"No, I didn't go into any of your things. I just checked the laundry basket. I hope that's okay."

The laundry basket had been in her room.

"Yes, of course. Sorry, I didn't mean to make a fuss. It's been a stressful day."

He gave her that lopsided smile, and a little of her anxiety faded away.

"Want to tell me about it?" he asked, his head tilted at an angle as he regarded her.

She cast a sideways glance to Ollie. "Maybe later."

She'd like that, spending a little time with Haiden, offloading about what had happened. He was completely impartial as far as the school was concerned, and she didn't need to worry about his gossiping to anyone. Of course, she knew it wasn't something she could get used to. Already, the weeks were flying by, and before she knew it, he'd have to leave, and she'd be all alone again.

Chapter Twenty-one

The crash of something breaking jolted her from sleep.

"Mummy!" Ollie's cry from his bedroom.

Instantly, she was awake and on her feet. What the hell had that been? It had sounded like something big breaking.

"Stay in your room, sweetheart," she called, stepping out into the hallway. "I'm just going to see what made the noise, okay?"

"I'm scared."

"It's nothing to be scared of. It was probably just Lemmy chasing a mouse around the kitchen."

That was what she was telling herself, but then why was her heart racing? She glanced at Haiden's closed bedroom door. Was he awake? Had he heard anything? It was the middle of the night. Surely, he'd have heard the crash, or her calling out to Ollie.

But no movement came from behind the door, and she couldn't go in there and wake him. He wasn't their personal bodyguard. Still, it would have been nice to have a big, strong man by her side, but then she reminded herself that she was an independent woman and more than capable of dealing with noises in the dead of night on her own.

She took the stairs quietly, placing her bare feet on the spots she knew wouldn't creak. She wished she had a weapon of some kind in her hand, just in case they were being broken into, but she hadn't even thought to pick up her phone in case she needed to call the police. No, she was overthinking things. The crash had been loud, but it probably was just Lemmy being an arsehole and knocking one of her vases or picture frames off the side.

She stepped into the kitchen, where it had sounded like the noise had come from. It felt cooler in here... and breezier. She frowned and moved further into the room.

"Ah, shit!" Pain lanced up through the bottom of her foot. She immediately stepped back again, but the damage had already been done. "What the hell?"

From what she could see, there was no one else in the room with her, but beyond the kitchen blinds gaped a space that had previously had glass in it... glass which was now all over the floor.

Kristen reached out, blindly finding the light switch on the wall.

Glass was everywhere, and in the middle of the glass sat a red brick. Her stomach plummeted. This had been done on purpose. Someone had picked up a brick and deliberately thrown it through the window.

Footsteps came from the stairs. "Mummy?"

"It's okay, baby. Don't come in here, though. There's glass all over the floor, and I don't want you to cut yourself."

"Why is there glass on the floor?"

"One of the windows broke."

"Why?"

"I'm not sure yet." She didn't want to tell him about the brick. Dammit. She was going to have to call the police now. She hadn't wanted to make a fuss, hoping this would all just go away, but she couldn't have someone smashing her windows in the middle of the night. Clearly, the same person who'd slashed her tyres had also done this. She hated to think that there was someone out there who hated her enough to try to scare her, but she couldn't deny that that was what was happening.

A male voice made her jump. "Kristen? Everything all right?"

She turned to find Haiden in the doorway. He only wore a pair of tracksuit bottoms, his chest bare. The noise she'd been making had obviously woken him, and he'd come straight down.

"Not really," she admitted.

He spotted the brick and frowned and opened his mouth to say something, but she shook her head and placed her fingers to her lips, trying to tell him that she didn't want Ollie to know. He seemed to understand what she was trying to say and gave her a nod.

She was mindful that she was only wearing a strappy little vest and a pair of jersey sleep shorts. She wasn't wearing any underwear and suddenly felt exposed. The broken window wasn't helping.

"You're hurt," he pointed out, nodding to her foot. Sure enough, red streaks of blood were smeared on the linoleum.

"It's nothing." She grabbed a kitchen towel and wadded it up against the sole of her foot.

"It's not nothing. You're bleeding." He reached out to her. "Let me take a look."

"I'm fine, honestly." She was aware of her son still sitting on the stairs and she didn't want to frighten him. "Let me get Ollie back to bed."

"Sure."

Still limping, and hoping she wasn't going to get any blood on the carpet, she left the room, brushing past Haiden's half naked torso, and went to her son still sitting on the stairs. "Come on, kiddo. Let's get you back to bed."

"How did the window break?" he asked, his voice small.

"Oh, I think naughty Lemmy must have knocked something into it," she lied.

With one hand on his shoulder, she guided him back to the bedroom, and he climbed back into bed. Right away, his eyelids began to droop.

She leaned in and kissed his smooth brow. "Haiden and I are just going to be tidying things up downstairs," she told him, "so don't worry if you hear more noises. It's only us."

"Okay, Mummy."

She could tell by his tone that he was already drifting. Another five minutes, and he'd be dead to the world.

She waited, sitting on the edge of his bed until it looked like he was asleep, and then got to her feet.

When she got downstairs, she discovered Haiden had already swept up most of the glass. The brick was sitting in the middle of the kitchen table like some alien lifeform that shouldn't be there.

"Oh, I was going to call the police," she said. "I wasn't sure if we should have touched anything until they arrived. This is a crime scene, after all."

Haiden put his fingers to his forehead. "Shit, sorry, Kristen. I didn't think."

"Did you touch the brick, too? It might have had fingerprints on it."

"Can you even get fingerprints from a brick?"

She shrugged. "I have no idea, but it seems like the logical place to start."

Deep down, she didn't want to get the police involved. She didn't want to be looked at as though she was making a fuss about nothing, but this had gone too far now. Whoever was trying to scare her—and it was working—was also scaring her son. Ollie had suffered enough with what was happening at school without him needing to be afraid when he was home as well.

But Haiden had swept up the glass now, and she was conscious of the time.

"Perhaps this can wait until the morning," she said, suddenly exhausted.

"Have you got a piece of board or something that I can put in the window for you?"

She regarded him gratefully. "Could you do that?"

"As long as you have something that'll fit and a nail gun, I'm sure I could manage it."

She almost wilted in relief. There was no way she'd have been able to sleep knowing that her kitchen window was a wide-open hole. Of course, anyone could just tear down a piece of board, but at least they wouldn't be so exposed.

Haiden left through the back door and returned carrying what he needed. Luckily, she'd never bothered to clear the shed out after Stephen had left, and though he'd taken some of his old tools, he'd left everything else. That had been one benefit of him feeling guilty for leaving her for another woman—other than the agreement to divide the sale of the house once Ollie had left full time education, Stephen had been happy to leave everything inside the house with her.

She helped Haiden get the piece of plyboard into position and flinched at the bang of each shot from the nail gun, hoping it wasn't going to wake Ollie again.

"There," he said, finally, standing back to admire his handiwork. "Now, how about I take a look at your foot?"

She'd almost forgotten about the cut. "It'll be fine, I'm sure."

"You might have glass stuck in it. Let me look." His tone was firm, and she didn't think she was going to get away with not letting him check it. Besides, a part of her longed for someone to take care of her, even if it was only for five minutes.

"Okay," she relented.

"Sit." He pointed at one of the kitchen chairs and she sank down into it.

"Where's your first aid kit?"

"In the cupboard under the sink."

He went to the kitchen sink and pulled open the cupboard door beneath it. He located the kit and brought it back to her, pulling up the chair opposite to face her. Scooping down, his fingers wrapped in a firm grip around her ankle and he tugged her injured foot into his lap.

Her breath caught, her heart beating harder. She was aware of how close her foot was to his groin, and a flash of the kiss they'd shared outside of the cinema burst into her head. He was only wearing a pair of low-slung tracksuit bottoms, his chest bare.

Apparently clueless to what was going on in her head, Haiden frowned down at her foot. He got to work, taking out some antiseptic wipes, plasters, and a bandage.

"I don't think it's going to need stitches," he told her. "Might be difficult to walk on while it's healing, though."

"It'll be fine. I'll manage."

His fingers pressed into the ball of her foot, and she wanted to groan in pleasure. She barely even remembered the cut—lost in the sensation of his muscular thigh beneath her calf, the touch of his fingers on her skin. She studied his handsome face while he focused on her foot.

Haiden glanced up and caught her staring. "Kristen..."

She sucked in a breath. The change between them was intense, as though invisible strings had joined them together and were now starting to pull. His hand left her foot, climbing up her calf and then her thigh, and then her waist. Without thinking, she followed her instincts and leaned into him, unable to resist.

They crashed together, their mouths meeting in frantic kisses. He tugged her off the chair and onto his lap, so she straddled him. She wrapped her hands around his neck, while he grabbed her bottom, grinding her against him.

God, he smelled so good, and felt incredible. Though in the back of her mind she knew this was wrong, and that Ollie could come down at any moment, after everything she'd been through, she didn't have the strength to push him away.

His kisses left her mouth, trailing across her jaw and down the side of her throat. Her nerve endings came alive, her skin buzzing at his touch. He yanked the bottom of her vest up, exposing her bare breasts, and threw the item of clothing to the floor. For once, she wasn't ashamed of how her breasts were no longer as perky as they'd once been, or that she had a roll of fat on her belly and stretch marks on her hips. Everything about him screamed that he wanted her, no matter her flaws, and his desire for her made her accept herself. She could feel how much he craved her pressing hard at the juncture of her thighs, and the pleasure of it made her heady with need.

Haiden palmed her breast and ducked his head, sucking her nipple into his mouth. She arched her back, pressing into him, wanting more. She ran her palms over the smooth curves of his muscles, marvelling at how he was both hard and soft at the same time.

He lifted his head from her breast, his blue eyes darkened with lust. "I want these off, too," he said, tugging at her shorts.

She knew what that meant. They were going to have sex.

He must have sensed her hesitation. "Shit, we don't have anything. You know, protection."

She could have used a lack of a condom as an excuse for getting out of this situation, but she wanted him. "Check the first aid box."

He arched one blond eyebrow. "You keep condoms in your first aid box?"

"I didn't!" Her cheeks burned. "Stephen did. He always used to get kind of frisky in the kitchen."

He pulled a face. "That was information I did not need to know."

"Sorry."

But he found what he was looking for, brandishing the foil packet, before pulling her in for another kiss. This time, his hands went to her shorts, and she lifted herself up so he could slide them down her thighs. She reached for him, too, the loose material of his jogging bottoms already tenting comically with his erection. Within a minute, they were both naked, and Haiden tore open the condom and rolled it down his length. He tugged her back into his lap, the position opening her to him, and she sank down onto him.

They moved together, slowly at first, their mouths joined, and then growing faster. Their kisses became frantic, their breathing fast and heavy. She slammed her hips down onto him and he lifted his from the chair to meet her.

The sex was fast and furious, and exactly what she needed. She reached her climax, her whole body shuddering with pleasure, her toes curling against the floor, her fingers digging into his shoulders. He groaned with her, and she felt him jerk inside her at his release.

They stayed together, catching their breath, their heart rates slowing.

Kristen knew they couldn't stay like this—still aware of Ollie asleep upstairs. She slid off Haiden and quickly grabbed her clothes and pulled them back on.

"Hey," he said, catching her hand. "Are you okay?"

She smiled and leaned in and kissed him. "Yeah, I'm great. That was kind of... unexpected."

"It certainly was." He paused then said, "Hey, Kristen, don't go saying this was a mistake in the morning, okay?"

"I won't," she assured him.

They crept off to their separate beds, hands held, exchanging kisses and goodnights. Kristen forced herself to let go of his fingers and walk away, even though they were only across the hall. She couldn't have Ollie waking up to find them in bed together. Not that there were many hours of the night left.

But as she fell asleep, she remembered the reason they'd both been down in the kitchen in the middle of the night, and the smile fell away from her lips.

Chapter Twenty-two

"**B**ut I'm tired!" Ollie's wail filled the house. "I don't wanna go to school!"

"You have to," Kristen said with a sigh, but she was already relenting. She was tired, too, and she really didn't want to have to walk up to school and face everyone. But she also knew how it would look to everyone if she called in and said Ollie was sick. They'd think she was sulking because of her suspension.

Kristen was torn.

Ollie let out a massive yawn and rubbed his hand over his bloodshot eyes. The poor kid did look exhausted. The thought of him being at school, emotional and over-tired, while Felix was still lording it up among all the boys was too much for her. Ollie's nose was still swollen across the bridge from where he'd been hit.

"Okay," she relented. "Let's have a sofa day."

A smile broke across his face, and her heart lifted.

"Really?" he said.

"Yeah, really. I have some things I need to take care of first, though, okay?"

"Can I watch the television?"

She didn't normally let him have TV during the week, but right now she needed him to be distracted so he didn't overhear the call she was putting in to the police about what had happened last night. Thinking of last night, her mind went to Haiden. He'd left first thing that morning, so they hadn't got a chance to talk, only exchanging a few stolen, knowing glances. A part of her was mortified that she slept with a man almost ten years her junior, and that he was a student she was supposed to be taking care of, but the other part of her fizzed with happiness.

With Ollie distracted, she called the school and told Anna that Ollie wouldn't be in today. Then she made the call to the police, using the local non-emergency number. She waited in a long queue and paced the house until she was eventually put through. To her disappointment, she was only given a crime reference number instead of the promises to send someone around that she was hoping for. It seemed the police had more important things to deal with than a broken window.

Shortly after she put the phone down, it rang again.

"Hello, Ms Scott, this is Duncan from the garage. Just calling to let you know that your car is ready."

"Oh, right. I'll try to come and pick it up at some point today. Thank you."

Now she needed to call her insurance company, and arrange a glazier, and pick up the car. It was a good thing she didn't have to go into work as well, or she'd have never got it all done. But deep down, she didn't want to do any of it.

Leaving the phone where it was, she went into the living room where Ollie was watching cartoons, his legs covered by a blanket. She climbed onto the opposite end of the sofa and wriggled her toes in underneath the throw to join him.

"What are we watching?" she asked him.

He named a show she'd never heard of before. Not that she even really cared what they were watching. Her head was filled with a jangle of thoughts, from Haiden to wondering who might be the person responsible for breaking her window and slashing her tyres.

A knock came at the front door, so she unravelled her legs from the blanket she was sharing with Ollie and went to answer it.

"Violet!" she exclaimed, opening the door to find her sister standing on the front step. "What are you doing here?"

Violet didn't wait to be invited in, but instead barged past her and into the living room.

"Hi, Ollie," she said, not sounding in the slightest bit surprised to see him lying on the couch, watching television.

"Hi, Aunty Vi," he replied, barely tearing his gaze from the screen.

Violet backed out, caught Kristen by the arm, and dragged her into the kitchen.

"What are you doing?" Kristen hissed, yanking back her arm.

"What am I doing?" she sounded incredulous. "What are *you* doing? I phoned the school trying to track you down since you haven't been answering any of my phone calls, and your friend, Anna, picked up. She told me what happened with that other mother, and that you'd called and said Ollie was sick this morning. He doesn't look very sick to me!" She caught sight of the boarded-up window. "And what happened to your kitchen window?"

"Don't you already know?" Her tone was hard. If Violet was the one responsible for all the things happening around her, then she'd already be well aware of her broken window.

Violet blinked in bafflement. "Why would I know?"

She pressed her lips together and shook her head. "Never mind. I'm not sure what happened. It broke during the night."

"Jesus." Violet looked back to Kristen. "So, what's going on with the school?"

She folded her arms, not even bothering to offer to make Violet a cup of tea. "Ollie is being bullied by another boy at school. An older boy. No one at the school is doing anything about it, which was why I had the fight with the boy's mother, and now I've been suspended. They're all corrupt up there, Violet. They're all in on it together. This mother, Rachelle, she heads up all the PTA stuff, and she'd practically snuggled right into the head teacher's pocket. No one has done anything to help Ollie, and I was at my wits' end. Yes, I might have gone too far, but what could I do?"

"And why is Ollie home now?"

She exhaled a long, deep sigh. "I didn't have the heart to send him in. He was crying this morning, saying he didn't want to go. He's finding it even harder now that I'm not there. I'm thinking of pulling him out, maybe even home schooling him while I try to find him a place at a different school."

Violet stared at her. "So, you're going to take him out of school and hole him up in this house with just you for company. Who does that remind you of?"

Kristen jerked back as though she'd been slapped. "This is nothing like she was!"

"Yeah, right. What's next? You already monitor his access to television like a hawk, you won't let him have any kind of games console or tablet—"

"He's five years old," she interrupted in disbelief. "Since when has it become normal for every five-year-old to have access to those kinds of things, and what makes you think it even should be that way?"

"Remember what Mum used to be like with us."

She snorted. "I could hardly forget!"

"She did everything she could to keep us away from the outside world, from all these things that could damage us, and look how that worked out. She wanted to keep us as little girls, trying to protect us from growing up, thinking that once we got older, we'd be exposed to more and more danger. Do you really think that did us any good?"

"This is nothing like Mum was. *I'm* nothing like Mum was!"

She thought back to her years growing up. They didn't do the stuff normal kids did. They didn't go out to fast food restaurants or even go to a normal secondary school, their mother insisting on home schooling them both. The only toys they were allowed were dolls, and stuffed teddies, and books. Even when she'd turned thirteen, her mother's gift to her had been a doll, and Kristen had been well over dolls by then. She'd craved makeup and CDs and concert tickets. She couldn't imagine what her mother would have been like if she'd been raising her and her sister in these days of the internet. She'd have lost her mind even quicker than she did. Things got worse when Kristen had started her periods. Her mother wouldn't even acknowledge that she needed sanitary products, laughing off her requests and saying things like 'you're too young to worry about that kind of thing.' Kristen, and then later Violet, had been reduced to using balled up wads of tissue paper or stealing their mother's supply, when they dared. On occasions, Kristen had even managed to sneak down to the corner shop, buying some with money she'd taken from her mother's purse, or even stealing the tampons—something she'd never been proud of.

The idea that she was putting her son through the same kind of childhood was ludicrous.

"You can just leave if you've only come here to accuse me of...of...I don't know... overprotecting my son!"

"What we went through wasn't overprotection, Kristen. You know that."

"Yes, and I also know that this situation isn't even remotely similar."

"I'm just worried about you, sis. And I'm worried about Ollie, too. You're shutting yourself off from more and more people. It's not even like you have any real friends."

Her mouth dropped open. How many times was Violet going to throw something unbelievable at her today? "What are you talking about? I have friends."

She shoved her hands on her hips, her eyebrow raised. "Who? Name a single one you could call in a crisis."

"Anna!" she declared. "I could call on Anna. She's always said for me to call her if I needed anything."

"Anna is a work colleague. How often do you see her outside of school hours, or anyone else, for that matter?"

"There are other mums who invite Ollie and me around for playdates," she protested. "They've invited me out for drinks and stuff as well."

"But you never go."

She slapped her hand down on the kitchen counter, suddenly frustrated. "Because I can never afford to! It's all right for you, Violet, lecturing me, but you have no idea what it's like to have the responsibility of looking after someone else. I've done it my whole life. I took care of you when we were younger and Mum was incapable, and then I had Ollie, and now I take care of him. I don't go out and see people because that all costs money, and unlike you, I don't want to drink my money away in expensive bars and pubs. I need to buy food, and clothes, and shoes—do you have any idea how expensive a decent pair of kids' school shoes are these days? His shoes cost twice the amount I spend on mine, and he seems to go through a pair every six months."

Her face burned and she was breathing hard, her heart galloping in her chest. All of this was so unfair. All she ever tried to do was the right thing for Ollie, and yet she was being attacked from every level. What the hell more did people expect from her? She felt as though if she opened a vein and bled for them, it still wouldn't be enough.

Since when had the tables turned so wildly? She was the one who had her life mostly sorted, and she was the one who was always picking Violet up, not the other way around.

"I think you need to go," she said, so angry she couldn't even look her sister in the eye.

Violet gave a hiss of exasperation. "Fine, but I'm only trying to look out for you both, remember that. Don't keep shutting everyone out, Kristen."

Violet spun away, shaking her head, and stormed from the room. Without even saying goodbye to her nephew, she slammed out of the front door.

Kristen put her face in her hands and tried not to cry. She was nothing like their mother—nothing! Their mum was paranoid someone was going to abduct the girls, that they'd be groomed by paedophiles and end up in a cellar owned by some perverted old man. Their mother's desperate attempt to both protect them from the outside world and try to pretend neither of them was really growing up into young women must have stemmed from somewhere, but neither she nor her sister had ever found out the cause of their mother's madness before she'd died. In later years, Kristen couldn't help but think their mum had been abused herself at some point during her childhood, and all she'd done was try to protect her two young daughters from going through the same, but she'd never spoken of it, and of course, things had gone way too far. Now, her mother had been dead for almost fourteen years, from a sudden brain haemorrhage, and they'd never get any answers. Kristen wasn't sure she even wanted to know. What good would it do to find out what their mother went through? It wasn't as though they could change anything now.

Movement came at the kitchen door, and Kristen swiped away her tears with the back of her hand, hoping Ollie hadn't seen them.

"What were you and Aunty Vi fighting about?" he asked, his bottom lip jutting out, his eyes round with worry.

"Oh, it was nothing, kiddo. Just grownup stuff."

"I heard you mention my name."

She put her arms out to him. "Come here." He stepped into her embrace and folded her son against her and squeezed him tight, leaning down to bury her nose in his soft, silky hair. "I was just explaining to your Aunty Vi that people who have children see things differently to people who don't." She released him slightly so she could look into his face. "You see, you are the most important person in my life, and it doesn't matter what else is going on, I will always think of you and what's best for you first. Your Aunty Vi doesn't get that. She thinks life should just be about having fun."

He risked a smile. "It's good to have fun."

"Yes, it is," she considered her words, "but not if that fun hurts someone else."

Chapter Twenty-three

It took her a while to calm herself down from her confrontation with Violet. Now she had a new thing to worry about. Was she starting to become her mother? It had never really been one of her fears, even after she'd had Ollie. The horror she'd been through as a teenager had been enough to convince her that she'd never turn out that way, but now Violet was putting ideas in her head. Could it be that she was going that way without even being conscious of it?

Another knock came at her door. It was still mid-morning, so she assumed it was the postman with something that wouldn't fit through her letter box. She put down the book she was reading and got up from the sofa to answer the door.

"Stephen!" The last person she'd been expecting to see was her ex-husband. He struggled to show up on the days they'd arranged, never mind the ones they didn't. "What are you doing here?"

"I heard you'd been suspended from work."

Immediately, she bristled. "How do you know that?"

"I spoke to Violet."

Fucking Violet.

"Well, you shouldn't have."

"I wouldn't have needed to if you'd been honest with me about what was going on with Ollie at school," he said, barging past her shoulder to enter the house. "She says you're talking about home schooling."

"It was just something that came up in conversation."

"What's wrong with you, Kristen? It's like you're not even stable anymore."

She wanted to retaliate with, *it's hardly surprising when someone is breaking my belongings and slashing my tyres.* But she kept her mouth shut. He'd have loved to have heard all of that. For all she knew, he was the one responsible for everything that was happening.

"I'm fine. I've just been standing up for our son, that's all."

"Daddy!" Ollie's voice came from the other room, and a second later he flew out of the door to hug Stephen.

"Hey, big guy," Stephen said, hugging him in return.

"Are you here to take me to your house?" Ollie asked.

It was an understandable train of thought, considering that was the only time Stephen was ever here.

"Nah, buddy," Stephen said. "Not today. I'm just here to talk to your mum."

"Everyone wants to talk to mum today," Ollie observed.

She forced a smile. "Guess I'm popular. Now give your dad and me a moment to chat, okay?"

Ollie let out a sigh and rolled his eyes. "Grownup stuff again." But he shuffled back into the lounge.

"Where's the other one?" Stephen asked, his gaze flicking up the stairs.

"By other one, I assume you mean Haiden?"

"Yeah, that's the one."

"He's in classes right now—not that it's any of your business."

Stephen gave a sigh, just like his son only moments earlier, and pushed his hand through his hair. "Look, Kristen, I was going to let this drop, but considering Ollie isn't even happy at school and you're not working there anymore..."

She lifted her hand to cut him off. "I've only been suspended, not fired. I have every intention of going back soon."

"When they let you, you mean."

Kristen scowled and folded her arms. "I know where you're going with this, and no, Ollie is not coming to live with you during the week so he can go to Lyla's school."

"Why not? It seems like the sensible choice. If he's not happy where he is, what's the point in making him stay there?"

"Because I'm his mother, and he needs me."

"Yeah, you're doing a really great job of that so far."

Rage surged up inside her. "How fucking dare you! You've been a part time father, at best. There's one little hiccup, and you think you can come charging in here and scoop him up. You're not taking my son away from me, do you hear me? I'll die before I let you."

He stared at her, shaking his head. "Jesus, Kristen. I always knew you were a little unstable when we were together, but this really takes the biscuit."

"Stop saying that! I am not fucking unstable!"

But right now, she felt unhinged. She clenched her hands by her sides and ground her teeth, doing everything in her power to stop herself from lunging at Stephen beating his chest with her fists.

"I'm just trying to be practical, Kristen. You're obviously a bit over-emotional right now, but give it some thought.

Perhaps, when you've calmed down, you'll see that what I'm suggesting makes sense."

"I will never let Ollie come and live with you during the week, do you understand me? Now get out of my house before I do something I regret."

Stephen shook his head, as though he was disappointed in her, and then leaned into the living room. "Bye, Ollie. I'll see you at the weekend, okay?"

"Bye, Daddy," the little voice filtered through.

Kristen bit back on a sudden desire to tell Stephen that he wouldn't get to see Ollie this weekend, or any other weekend any time soon. Though the urge to be vicious and try to hurt lay within her, she knew she never wanted to be that kind of parent. It would be all too easy to use Ollie as a weapon, but the main person who'd get hurt was him. She loved her son too much to do that.

Stephen finally left, and she shut the door on him, and then pressed her back against it, shaking. She didn't know how much more she could take today. Since when had she become everyone's enemy?

Was this Stephen's way of getting Ollie for good? Was he doing things to her home and car to try to make her look incapable of taking care of him? Her mind went to the letter from the solicitor. Had Stephen been advised to do these things to her in order to get custody of Ollie?

Whatever he was playing at, she had no intention of letting him win.

THAT EVENING, HAIDEN didn't come home at his normal time.

As the minutes ticked past, she grew more and more anxious about why he was late. She checked her phone, making sure she hadn't missed a call or message from him, and wondered if she should send him a message instead. There were no guidelines for this situation, and she didn't want to look as though she was chasing him. Of course, it was just manners for him to let her know if he wasn't coming home for dinner, but other than that, he was free to do whatever he wished. Just because they'd slept together didn't mean they were in any kind of relationship. Maybe now that he'd shagged his landlady, he was on the hunt for someone younger, and had taken someone he'd met at the university out, instead. God, if he paraded some perky eighteen-year-old around, she thought she might die.

Her heart was heavy, and her insides churned like she'd eaten something that hadn't agreed with her. She wished she could take back them having sex, but that was impossible.

The front door clicked open, and she froze. Would he go straight upstairs, or come looking for her? Would he even mention what they'd done, or perhaps it would be better if they both acted like it had never happened? He'd said he hadn't wanted for her to say them having sex had been a mistake, but he'd been high on the moment and endorphins when he'd said that. Things always looked different in the cold light of day.

The kitchen door opened, and she forced a smile. Haiden looked exactly like he always did—handsome and relaxed. She'd probably spent the day agonising over everything, while he'd barely given what they'd done a second thought.

"Hey," he said. "Sorry I'm late. I had something I needed to take care of."

"That's okay. No problem."

He crossed the room and came up behind her. To her surprise, he wrapped his arms around her waist and nuzzled her neck. "I haven't stopped thinking about last night all day."

Her stomach flipped, her breath catching. "You haven't?"

He spun her in his arms, so she was facing him.

"Of course not." He must have sensed her hesitation as he leaned back to see into her face. "You're not having regrets, are you?"

She shook her head. "Not regrets, no, but I'm not sure it can happen again."

Oh, but how she wanted it to. Just being in such proximity to him made her feel like she was alive again, like she could forget all the other shit that was being thrown at her.

"We're both adults, Kristen. I know it's not a usual setup, but neither of us are doing anything wrong."

"The university..." she started, but even she could hear that her heart wasn't in her protests.

"There's no reason for them to find out. In fact, I'm not even sure about the course I'm doing there anymore. It isn't what I was expecting."

"It isn't?"

"No, I'm not really enjoying it."

"But if you leave, you won't be covered by the university housing anymore."

"Exactly."

Her mind was spinning. "So, you'd have to move out?"

"Or you just stop being a host for them."

This was all getting a bit much. "We've only known each other a few weeks, Haiden. I'm not sure I can rush into big decisions like this. I've got a lot on my plate right now, what with everything happening at school, and then Stephen, Ollie's father, stopped by earlier and threatened to make things difficult for me. He'd use any excuse to make me look like a bad mother, and he'd somehow twist around how I'm sleeping with a student, even if you are a mature one."

Haiden's expression darkened, his eyes growing hard. "Stephen's been hassling you? He was around here?"

"Yes, but I dealt with it. As I'm sure you're aware, I'm an adult."

"Yes, you are," he agreed, "which is why you shouldn't let people push you around."

He swept the hair away from her neck and placed a kiss at the point where her neck met her shoulder, sending shivers of pleasure through her.

She knew she shouldn't let people push her around, but it seemed like Haiden had a whole other way of getting what he wanted.

Chapter Twenty-four

The next day, she pulled herself together and took Ollie to school. She kept an eye out for Rachelle and Felix, but there was no sign of either of them in the playground. While she was happy not to go through any awkward confrontations, she did think it was strange. Rachelle was one of those women who was always on time, and never forgot P.E. kits or to sign forms that were needed for some activity or another. That they weren't here when school started was unusual, and she hoped Rachelle's absence wasn't anything to do with her.

She caught Anna's eye across the long line of parents who were already trailing out of the office door. She was annoyed with Anna for telling Violet what had happened. That hadn't been Anna's place, and she wanted to say something, but knew she couldn't do it in front of everyone like this. People would be gossiping about her already. She had no intention of stoking the fire.

Giving Ollie a kiss goodbye, she left the school to hurry home. She needed to go and pick up the car, complete with four new tyres and a large bill, and the glazier was due to come around to fix the window as well. Though the chores were annoying, she was at least grateful she wasn't going to spend the day at a loose end, overthinking things, as usual.

Haiden had kissed her before he'd left that morning. The small gesture of affection had made her feel like they were approaching an actual relationship. He was the one thing that was going well in her life, and even though, deep down, she knew it couldn't possibly go anywhere, she couldn't bring herself to stop.

Her phone rang, and she frowned down at the name displayed. It was Anna. Anna rarely phoned her unless it was to do with something at work, and it wasn't as though it could be that, since she hadn't even been there. She hoped this wasn't going to have something to do with Violet sticking her nose in.

She picked up the phone and swiped green to answer. "Anna, hi?"

Anna didn't even bother saying hello. "Have you heard?"

"Heard what?"

"Felix Hurst has been in an accident."

"Oh my God." She sank down onto one of the kitchen chairs. "Is he okay? What happened?"

"It sounds like he was climbing a tree in their back garden yesterday evening and fell. He's badly injured his spine. He's in hospital. They're not sure he's going to be able to walk again."

"Oh, shit." She clamped her hand over her mouth. "That's terrible."

Automatically, she couldn't help but put herself and Ollie in that position, imagining it was Ollie badly hurt and lying in a hospital bed. Those kinds of accidents could happen to anyone. There was no love lost between herself and Rachelle Hurst, but as one mother to another, she could empathise and feel terrible for the other woman. The amount of fear and worry going through Rachelle's head right now must be heartbreaking.

"Yeah, it is. Poor them," Anna said, though she didn't sound particularly sympathetic.

"Is the school going to do something for them?" Kristen asked. "A card and collection to take to the hospital?"

"Not that I know of, but it's a good idea. I'll run it by Andrew tomorrow and see what he thinks. He's always been a fan of Rachelle's, so I'm sure he'll be one hundred percent behind doing something. Hell, he'll probably organise it himself."

She allowed herself a smile, though it contained a hint of bitterness. "Yeah, you're probably right."

"I'll tell him that it was your idea, though, Kristen. You know, now that there's not much chance of Felix coming back to school any time soon, and I'm sure Rachelle will have her hands full with taking care of him, maybe I could mention to Andrew that it would be a good idea to bring you back from your suspension sooner rather than later. Rachelle's going to be too busy to even notice, never mind kick up a fuss, and Felix won't be here, so you won't have to worry about any more run-ins."

Go back to work?

She wasn't sure how she felt about that. Of course, she needed the money, but a part of her had enjoyed not having to put Ollie in breakfast and afterschool club and being able to pick him up with all the other mothers. She also felt bad at the idea of benefitting off a tragic accident, though the thought of being at school and not needing to worry about where Felix was in relation to Ollie or having to put up with death stares from Rachelle across the playground also lifted a weight from her shoulders.

"That would be great, Anna. Thanks."

"Honestly, I think he'll jump at the chance of getting you back if Rachelle's no longer around to pile on the pressure. It's been a nightmare here since you left, and all the teachers and parents are complaining."

"They couldn't find anyone to fill in for me, then?"

"Nope, it's the job no one else wants."

She laughed at that. "Well, if you could let Andrew know I'm motivated to come back, that would be great, and that I've learned my lesson, of course." She hoped the spots at breakfast and afterschool club were still open.

"Sure."

"And I am sorry to hear about Felix. Let me know if there's a collection or anything." She wasn't sure she had much to spare, but if she got her job back, the pressure was off. Hopefully, no one at the university would find out about her and Haiden, and she'd continue to receive that money, too.

"Will do," Anna chirped. "Chat later."

She hung up.

Kristen finished her chores for that day, and then went to pick Ollie up from school at three. She wondered how much the children had been told about what had happened to Felix, and wished she'd asked Anna when she'd had the chance. She decided not to mention anything to him unless he brought it up. She didn't know how he was going to react, and she didn't want to upset him unnecessarily.

But as soon as they got into the house, Ollie turned to her. "What's happened to Felix?"

"Let's sit down for a minute," she said, putting out her arms to him.

He went to her, and she took a seat at the kitchen table, pulling him onto her lap, taking comfort in his solid weight and warmth. It was easy to take the health and safety of her son for granted at times, but Felix's accident reminded her that having Ollie was a gift, and even the times when she was tired and angry and frustrated, and he kept getting out of bed, or wanted just one more drink of water, and insisted on one more story, that there were plenty of mothers out there who would carve out their own hearts just to give their child one last kiss before bedtime.

"Felix has had a bit of an accident."

He gazed up at her with wide, trusting eyes. "What happened?"

"He fell out of a tree and hurt his back, and now he's going to have to spend some time in hospital."

"I hope he's okay."

"Yeah, me too, baby, but in the meantime, he's not going to be at school."

"Does that mean you're coming back?" Excitement lifted his voice.

"I'm not sure yet. We have to wait and see." She paused and asked, "Do you want me back at school?"

"Yeah!" he enthused, twisting around to throw his small arms around her neck.

She smiled and hugged him back. "Even if it means going to breakfast and afterschool club again?"

He released her and shrugged. "I don't mind. It means I get to play for longer."

"Yes, you do. Well, we'll have to wait and see what your headteacher says, okay?"

"Okay."

He remained on her lap, and she could tell he wanted to say something.

"What is it, kiddo?"

He let out a long sigh. "Was it because of me that you weren't allowed to do your work anymore?"

"Hey! No, not at all! What made you think that?"

Ollie shrugged. "'Cause you got into a fight with Felix's mummy, and then you got sent home. But I knew you got into that fight because of me."

She wriggled him around so she could look into his face. "Listen to me. It was not your fault. Felix was badly behaved, and the grownups didn't do what was needed to make sure he learned the right way to behave. But the other grownups didn't agree with me, and that's why I got sent home. It was all about the grownups, not you kids. Not even Felix, okay?"

He twisted his lips and nodded. "Okay."

"And anytime you have questions like that, just come and ask me. I'm not going to be angry with you for asking questions."

"Can I ask another one, then?"

"Of course."

"How much longer is Haiden going to be staying?"

She frowned at the sudden change of subject. "Haiden? Why? Don't you like having him here?"

"I don't know. Sometimes, I wish it was just the two of us again."

"Oh, sweetheart, he's still going to be here for another couple of months. I know it's different having someone else around, but we really need the money."

Guilt speared at her heart. This was parenting in a nutshell. She felt guilty when they didn't have any money. Guilty when she was working. Guilty when she wasn't. And now she had to feel guilty about pushing a stranger into Ollie's life as well. Did Ollie realise there was something more between her and Haiden? They'd done their best not to let him see any of the secret touches and kisses, but perhaps the atmosphere had changed between them?

"The time will fly by, I promise," she told him.

But even as the words left her mouth, she worried she wouldn't want to see Haiden go.

Chapter Twenty-five

The front door slammed, and heavy footsteps pounded up the stairs.

Kristen winced at the sound, pausing stirring the chilli she was making for dinner. Haiden was home, and the volume of the noise he was making to announce his arrival told her he wasn't happy about something.

Perhaps she would have left him alone before they'd slept together, but now she felt like he might need her in more of a capacity than simply providing a roof over his head and meals on the table. If something was bothering him, she wanted him to confide in her.

She turned down the heat under the chili and climbed the stairs. That familiar buzz of a phone ringing while it was on silent filtered through his bedroom door, and she frowned, wondering why he never answered it. What had happened with his family before he'd left that made him not want to speak to them?

Lifting her hand, she knocked lightly on the door. "Haiden? Is everything okay?"

His gruff voice came back to her through the wood. "I'm fine."

"Can I speak to you? You're worrying me."

To her alarm, the door flew open, and he stood in the space, dwarfing it. "Not everything has to be about you, Kristen," he snapped, his blue eyes hard.

She drew back, suddenly intimidated by his size. She wasn't used to this. He'd never made her feel this way before.

"No, I'm... I'm sorry. I didn't mean to turn things around to me. I was just worried about you. That's all I meant. Something has clearly upset you."

He slammed his fist against the side of the doorframe, and she jumped. "It's this damned course I'm doing. It's not what I was expecting."

"It isn't?" This wasn't the first time he'd mentioned that he was struggling. She'd hoped things had got better, but they clearly hadn't improved.

"No, the knowledge I'm expected to have doesn't tie in with what they're running. We're having a bit of a..." he paused as he searched for the right word. "Disconnect."

"Oh, I'm sorry." What did this mean? Would he be looking to leave early? She didn't know how she felt about that. Not only did she not want to lose the money from his housing, she also didn't want him to leave either. "Do you think you'll be able to sort it out?"

Haiden exhaled a sigh, and his shoulders relaxed. He reached out and laced his fingers through hers, and excitement danced through her at the contact. She wished she didn't have such an instant reaction to him, but she'd been starved of any kind of affection for years now, and suddenly there was this handsome man in her home, and he genuinely seemed to like her.

"I don't know. Everyone there seems so different to me. Honestly, you're the only person I've made any kind of connection with since I arrived in the UK."

"Are people not being friendly? I thought there were plenty of others from other countries studying with you?"

"There are." Another sigh escaped his lips. "Maybe it's just that the only person I want to be around right now is you."

He tugged her towards him. She was aware of Ollie in his bedroom, reading on his bed, but she couldn't help smiling. "Haiden..."

He pressed himself closer, the fronts of their bodies grazing. "What?"

She still didn't pull away, but tilted her head to the side, gazing up at him from beneath her eyelashes. "You know what."

Ollie stepped out of his bedroom, and they jumped apart.

Instantly, she spun towards her son. "Hey, sweetie. Everything all right?"

"I'm hungry," Ollie complained. "When's dinner?"

"Soon. I'm just finishing it up now."

She exchanged a glance with Haiden, who threw her a wink. The tension that had been between them dissipated. He wasn't angry with her or doubting their relationship. This was purely about his education.

They ate dinner together, and once they were sure Ollie was finally sound asleep, they curled up together on the sofa in the pretence of watching television but spent most of the evening making out like a couple of teenagers. Kristen constantly had one ear out for any sign of movement upstairs, but with Haiden this close, there was no way she could resist. She put out of her mind how intimidated she'd been when he'd been standing in the bedroom doorway, and the hard look to his eyes.

Haiden had become like a drug, and she was well and truly addicted.

KRISTEN WOKE WITH A start.

Realising the time, she exclaimed in annoyance. She'd stayed up too late with Haiden the previous evening and had slept in late.

She hated that frantic moment where she realised the morning was going to be a rush now to get Ollie to school on time. Ollie hated being rushed, too, and she knew there were going to be tears before she'd even managed to leave the house.

If only Haiden had knocked on her bedroom door before he'd left for classes that morning. He must have realised she'd overslept.

Perhaps he figured she needed some rest after all the physical exertion.

She pressed a smile between her lips at the memory.

Working on fast forward, she got Ollie out of bed and shoved some breakfast at him, half throwing on his clothes while he ate. Her breakfast could wait until she got back from the school drop off. She wondered if she might hear from Andrew about her suspension today.

They made it to school, scraping in on the bell, and Kristen kissed her son goodbye and hurried home again. She'd barely managed to brush her hair before she'd left the house and was dying for a cup of tea.

Her home phone was ringing as she walked in the door, so she rushed to pick it up. "Hello?"

"Is that Kristen?"

It was a female voice—one she recognised but couldn't quite place. "Yes, it is. Who's this?"

"Kristen, it's Lisa. Stephen's wife. New wife, I mean."

Her stomach twisted. "Lisa? Is everything okay?"

Lisa never called. She'd spoken to her on the odd occasion where Kristen had called the house when Ollie was staying over there, but that was all. They'd never really had a proper conversation about anything other than Ollie and a couple of passing niceties.

"No, it's not," Lisa said. "I'm afraid Stephen—" Her voice suddenly sounded strangled, and alarm jumped inside Kristen.

"Stephen what? What's happened?"

"He's been hit by a car," she sobbed. "He was out on his run this morning, and he didn't come home when he was supposed to. I got worried, but then the police turned up and said he was in hospital. Someone found him on the side of the road and called an ambulance."

"Oh my God. Is he going to be okay?"

"We don't know yet. He's suffered a head injury and it looks like some broken bones as well."

"Jesus. Do they know who hit him?"

"No, the bastard just left him there for dead."

Her world spun, and she lowered her head, trying to make sense of what Lisa had told her. Stephen had been involved in a hit and run. While she had no love for him anymore, she'd never have wanted him to be hurt. Her heart tightened as she realised she'd have to tell Ollie his daddy was in hospital.

"What can I do to help?" she finally managed to say.

"Nothing, really. My mum is taking the kids, so I can be with him."

"What about Ollie? Should I bring him in?"

"No, don't. Stephen's got tubes coming out of his nose and mouth, and he isn't awake. It's not a pretty sight, and I think it would only scare the children."

"Yes, of course. Stupid of me."

"Not at all. I've had a couple of hours to get my head around what's happened. This is brand new to you. I wasn't thinking straight at first. Thank God for my parents—they came over immediately."

"You're lucky to have them." Crazily, she discovered herself to be jealous of a woman whose husband had just been involved in a hit and run. She shook the thought out of her head. "Please, will you let me know if there are any changes? And if you need anything at all, don't hesitate to ask. I mean it, Lisa."

"Thanks, Kristen. That's kind of you."

"It's the least I can do."

They said goodbye, with promises to keep in touch, and then Kristen sank down onto the sofa. She felt shaky and distanced from her surroundings, as though nothing was quite real.

Stephen was badly hurt. What would she do if he died?

She ran back over what had been said, making sure she hadn't missed anything.

If Lisa had already had a couple of hours to let the news sink in, the accident must have happened early. Sometime between six and seven in the morning, she guessed. Christ, since when did Stephen start jogging? He never jogged when they were together.

She suddenly felt horribly alone.

Reaching for her mobile phone, she typed in a message.

Something has happened. I need you.

And then she sat back and tried to figure out how she was going to break the news of Stephen's accident to their son.

Chapter Twenty-six

Kristen opened the door to her sister.

"Oh my God, Kristen," Violet said, opening up her arms to scoop Kristen into them. "I came straight here. I'm so sorry about Stephen. Are you okay? Do they know what happened?"

Kristen sagged into Violet's embrace and choked back a sob. Violet had responded as soon as she'd sent the message, and after Kristen had told her about Stephen, she'd dropped everything to come over.

"I'm so sorry about all those things I said the other day," Violet continued. "I don't know what got into me. You're a great mum, and I know you'll make the right choices for Ollie."

She shook her head. "No, you were right. I was taking it too far. Ollie loves school. He'd be miserable if he had to stay home with me all day, and besides, it's not teaching him how to deal with his problems if I'm just hiding him away from them. You were right to say I was taking a leaf out of Mum's book of parenting."

"So, we're okay?" she asked with a cautious smile.

Kristen smiled back and put out her arms. "Of course."

The two sisters hugged each other hard, then they went into the kitchen and sank down into chairs at the table.

"So, is Stephen going to be okay?" Violet asked cautiously.

"We don't know much yet. He's got a fractured skull, and broken arm and ribs. Looks like the top half of his body took most of the impact."

"My God." She placed her fingers to her lips. "Do they know who did it yet?"

"Nope. No clue. It was a quiet road, and he was out jogging. Someone hit him from behind and just took off. Luckily, someone else came along not long after and called an ambulance."

"I've never been a fan of Stephen's, but I wouldn't wish that on anyone. It must have been terrifying, lying there, hurt and not able to do anything about it."

Kristen grimaced. "I know. Hopefully, he won't remember much of that part, though."

"What are you going to do about Ollie? Are you going to take him in to see his dad?"

Kristen pulled a saltshaker towards her, twisting it in her fingers as a distraction. "No, there's no point in frightening him. And it's not as though he'd have seen Stephen this week anyway, so he doesn't know any different. I'd rather he goes to see him when Stephen is doing better. If there's machines and tubes and stuff, I don't think Ollie would handle it too well."

She nodded. "I understand. You're making the right choice."

"I hope so."

Kristen let out a sigh and put her head in her hands. She was so tired—tired of everything. Tired of fighting all the time. She felt as though she'd been doing it her whole life and right now, she'd had enough. She wanted to walk away and start again, but she couldn't do that. She had Ollie to think of, and so, even though she was exhausted, and nothing ever seemed to be good enough, she'd wake up tomorrow and start fighting all over again.

Violet's wrapped her fingers around Kristen's arm and gave her a squeeze. "Hey, you're doing a great job, and everything will be all right."

She lifted her gaze to her sister. "If you keep saying that, will it make it true?"

"You bet."

The two sisters smiled at each other.

Kristen heard the click of the front door opening and turned at the sound. The kitchen door pushed open, and Haiden appeared around the corner. He spotted the two women and their serious expressions and frowned.

"Kristen, what's wrong? Is it Ollie?"

She stood to greet him. "No. It's Stephen. He's been involved in a hit and run. He's badly hurt." Her voice broke on the last sentence and Haiden's look of concerned deepened.

"Oh, shit." He pulled her into his arms, his hands in her hair, her face pressed to his chest. The heat of his breath warmed the top of her head.

Aware that Violet was still sitting at the table, she pulled away and glanced over at her sister. She caught the knowing look Violet gave her. Well, that was one cat out of the bag. Not that it mattered now, she guessed. There were bigger things to worry about.

Chapter Twenty-seven

The next few days passed in a blur.

She broke the news to Ollie after he'd finished school that same day.

Ollie had looked up at her, his eyes wide with worry and confusion. "So, Daddy and Felix both had a bad accident?"

Her heart sank. Of course, she hadn't even thought about Felix. Did that make her a horrible person? Now, poor Ollie had two people in his life who'd been badly hurt. Things like people getting seriously hurt, or even killed, were theoretical to five-year-olds. Sometimes they didn't even really understand what it all meant until it happened to someone close, and even then, they had trouble comprehending what it meant for the future.

"Yes, but they're completely different accidents. It's just bad luck, that's all."

"Is Daddy going to be all right?"

"He's got the best doctors looking after him right now, so you don't have to worry at all, okay?"

She hadn't really answered his question, but she didn't want to directly lie to him. She couldn't say for sure that Stephen was going to be all right, but it wasn't as though she was going to tell Ollie that. She bit back tears at the possibility of having to tell Ollie his father had died. The idea of being the cause of such pain for her son was unbearable. She prayed it wouldn't come to that.

Luckily, Stephen had taken Ollie the previous weekend, so Ollie wasn't expecting to go to his dad's again. Due to Stephen's erratic schedule, Ollie didn't really know any different when it came to his father not being around. Of course, Ollie had asked to see his dad, but she'd told him that his dad was busy with the doctors. It broke her heart that Ollie had heard about his dad being too busy to see him so often that the boy simply accepted the excuse.

Later that day, the police found the car they suspected to be used in the hit and run. The owner of the car had reported it stolen around seven in the morning. It was after the hit and run had occurred, but the police believed it was simply because the owners hadn't been awake to notice the car missing, and there was no reason to think they were involved in any way. They still had no idea who'd been driving the car. It appeared to have been wiped clean of prints after it had been dumped.

Stephen woke up after three days, but he was far from out of the woods. He'd suffered some swelling on his brain that affected his speech, and the pain medication they'd given him for his injuries didn't help. Kristen went in to see him while Ollie was at school and was shocked at how bad he'd looked. She'd barely recognised him—covered in tubes and bandages—and he hadn't seemed to know who she was either. His speech had been slurred, and he'd barely looked at her.

Lisa was by his side the whole time. "He doesn't remember what happened," she told Kristen. "It might come back to him, but it might not. The doctors say it's pretty common to block it out."

"But they think he's going to be all right?"

"Yes, he's out of the woods now. It's going to take some time, but we're over the worst of it."

She reached out and took Lisa's hand. "He's lucky to have you," she said, genuinely meaning it. Lisa seemed calm and together, and totally devoted to Stephen. She wasn't sure Stephen deserved to have someone like Lisa, but perhaps this accident would make him realise how blessed he was to have such an amazing woman who clearly loved him.

That afternoon, she went home and cried all over again. Cried in relief that Stephen was going to be okay, cried with relief that Ollie wasn't going to lose his father, and cried at the prospect of the uncertainty of her near future while Stephen was recovering. She hadn't wanted to mention anything to Lisa—aware the other woman had more than enough on her plate—but she wondered if she'd still be receiving maintenance payments. Plus, she could hardly expect either Stephen or Lisa to take Ollie for any time until Stephen was better. She was most definitely doing this on her own for the foreseeable future.

Both Violet and Haiden had been brilliant since the accident. Violet was helping out with Ollie, since she was between yet another temp job and didn't have anywhere else to be. Haiden had been caring and supportive, but neither of them could take away the emotional burden she carried.

After she got back from the hospital, she put her head in her hands and let out a sigh.

Haiden regarded her. He'd been coming home earlier and earlier from the university, and she had the feeling he wasn't even going to classes anymore, but she didn't have it in her to deal with his issues with his course as well.

"I think you need a break," he said. "This has all been too much for you."

She sniffed. "I can't afford a break."

He sat back, twisting his lips as he thought. "You know, one of the other students I'm doing my masters with is even older than me."

"And?" The weariness in her voice was clear. She didn't want to listen to any problems he might be having in his course.

He held up a hand. "Let me finish. He's got a family holiday cottage up on the moors. He's often talked about how they rent it out. Let me see if he'll rent it out to me, and we'll take the weekend up there. Away from this place, and all the people, and the school. Just the two of us."

She couldn't imagine that—not having to think about anyone else for an entire weekend. Just the idea made the weight lift from her shoulders.

"I think I'd really like that. It would be good for me." She realised what he'd said about it just being the two of them. "What about Ollie?"

"Won't your sister have him? It'll only be for one night."

She nodded. "I'll ask."

Things had been better between her and Violet since Stephen's accident. It would only be one night, wouldn't it? She felt bad at leaving Ollie, but he hadn't been badly affected by his father's accident. Things might be different if Stephen was a full-time father, but since Ollie hadn't seen the extent of his injuries yet, the boy was getting on with things as usual.

When Violet popped around to see how she was doing, she broached the subject. Violet was fully aware that Kristen and Haiden's relationship was more than just host and student by now, but she'd known better than to comment on it.

"Haiden wants us to have a night away. Apparently one of his fellow mature students has a little cottage up on the moors. He thinks it'll do me good to get away."

Violet nodded. "I agree. It will. I'll take Ollie for the night. He can stay with me, or I'll come and stay here—whichever you prefer. I'll be happy to spend some time with him."

Kristen pulled a face, her insides twisting. "How can I just leave him when his dad's been in an accident?"

"You said yourself that he's completely unaware how bad the accident was. Ollie's fine."

"I know, but ..." She trailed off.

"Well, then. Decision made."

The idea of getting away from this place did appeal. Too much had been happening, and it would be wonderful being somewhere different with Haiden—somewhere she didn't have to worry about someone seeing them together. She was completely drained by the events of the last few weeks, and she needed some time to recharge. She'd be able to come back refreshed and be a better mum for Ollie.

"Thanks, Violet. I don't know what I'd do without you."

Chapter Twenty-eight

H aiden slammed down the boot of the car. "Ready?"
Kristen smiled and nodded. "Yeah, I'm ready."

Though they were only going for one night, she'd packed enough changes of clothes and underwear to last a week. There was a pub about a mile's walk from the cottage, where they planned to go for dinner and a couple of drinks before walking back again. Once they were back, she hoped they'd spend the rest of their time together in bed. It had been a long time since she'd felt like this about someone, and she tried to ignore the niggling voice in her head telling her not to get used to it. He was going home in a couple of months, and this would all be over, whether she liked it or not. There was no point in talking about long distance relationships either. Haiden was young and gorgeous, and he deserved better than being tied to a single mother in her thirties who lived a thousand miles away.

She gave Ollie what she hoped would be a reassuring smile and ruffled his hair.

"Are you sure you're going to be all right?" she asked Violet, anxious to be leaving without him.

"Of course. We're going to have loads of fun, aren't we, Ollie? I've got some age inappropriate films for us to watch, and a bucket full of popcorn, and all washed down with ice-cream sodas."

"Yay!" Ollie cheered, clapping.

"Well, you're going to have fun with him when he's climbing the walls," Kristen said with a laugh.

"I'm only kidding. We're having sushi, and I'll have him in bed by seven."

Kristen didn't know which version to believe. "Okay, as long as you both have fun. That's the main thing."

"We will, I promise."

"And you won't forget to feed Lemmy, either?"

Violet gave her an exasperated glare. "If I can remember to feed your son, I'm sure I can handle the cat."

Kristen gave Ollie another hug and a kiss and told him to be good, and then hugged her sister. Haiden was waiting beside the passenger side of the car. She turned and gave him a smile. He nodded in return and climbed into the passenger seat. The tyres were all new—or at least new to the car—so they were good to go.

Since she was the only one on the insurance, Kristen drove. She watched her little family disappearing in the rear-view mirror, trying to quell her anxiety about leaving them, and then forced herself to focus on the road.

The cottage was an hour's drive away. As they increased the distance between her and home, she felt like she could finally breathe.

"I can hardly believe we're doing this," she said, glancing over at Haiden's profile as she drove. "It feels completely crazy."

He smiled over at her. "Nothing crazy about two people meeting and falling for each other."

"I know, but if you'd told me a few weeks ago, when you first stepped off the coach, that we'd be doing this, I would have told you that you'd lost your mind."

"No one's lost their minds, Kristen."

"No, I know that." His tone was strange. Was it because of what Violet had said about their mother and her mental health issues? He was just being protective of her, and probably didn't want her to head down that same path.

She glanced over at him again to make sure everything was all right, and he flashed her another of those perfect, white smiles. She was overthinking things, as usual. Reading too much into a simple, throwaway comment. But she did hope he didn't think she was unstable at all.

The car ate the miles, and before she knew it, they were off the motorway and onto the narrow, single lane tracks of the countryside. She slowed to cross over a grate designed to stop the wild ponies and sheep from leaving the moorland, and then had to pull in to allow another vehicle through that was coming in the opposite direction.

"This is stunning," she said, when she pulled back out again. There was no sign of houses, or any other kind of buildings, for that matter. Fluffy white clouds appeared painted onto the blue expanse of sky. Little copses of trees were dark patches against the yellow gorse of the moors.

"Yes, it is. It's not too far away from where you live, either. Do you not come up here much?"

She shook her head. "No. I think we might have visited as children, but I can't really remember. I don't know this area at all."

"I think you'll really love it. It's totally secluded. It'll just be the two of us for once, no one on the outside peering in."

"You said there's a pub not far away."

"That's right. It's about a mile or so away, but it's supposed to be a nice walk."

She laughed. "I think I can manage to walk a mile."

"And back again," he pointed out.

"As long as I don't drink too much while we're there, of course. Then you might have to carry me back."

He threw her a wink. "I think I can manage that."

The idea of him throwing her over his shoulder like some rough, big Viking gave her a little thrill of excitement. She was so lucky to be doing this, but with her happiness came a pang of guilt. It had been a long time since she'd taken any kind of holiday, even if it was only for one night, and she was doing it while her ex-husband was lying in a hospital bed.

"I feel bad that we left Ollie behind," she admitted. "He probably can't even remember the last holiday we took."

Haiden reached out and took her hand. He squeezed her fingers, just a little too tight, and she frowned down at their joined hands. "You don't have to worry about Ollie all the time, Kristen. You're allowed to exist without him. *We're* allowed to exist without him."

"Well, yes, but he is my son."

She pulled her fingers from his grip, and a little worm of unease wiggled through her. She dismissed it. Haiden was allowed to want her all to himself, wasn't he? Of course, she and Ollie came as a package, and he'd been nothing but great with Ollie this whole time. But now they were supposed to be having a night away as a couple for the first time ever, and she could hardly blame him for getting irritated by going on about her son.

"Sorry," she said, throwing him an awkward smile. "I'll stop mentioning Ollie all the time."

"No, it's fine. He's your son, I know that. I'm just being selfish for wanting you all to myself. Besides, you're allowed to enjoy yourself without him and not feel guilty about it. I bet he's having a brilliant time with Violet."

She exhaled a long sigh. "You're right. I know you are." Even so, she glanced down to where her phone sat in one of the cup holders. The reception was patching out here, but a bar flashed up, and there were no missed calls or messages. Haiden was right. Ollie was probably having the time of his life with her sister. It would be doing him good, too, to have her take his mind off everything.

"We're almost there," Haiden said. "I think that must be the local pub."

She craned her neck to see a pretty, thatched pub with a river running through the gardens, picnic tables positioned outside. It was approaching lunchtime, and there were already a couple of cars in the car park. She had a sudden longing for a doorstep sandwich and half a pint of lager.

They continued past, leaving her dreams of lunch behind her. She'd noticed Haiden had packed them a picnic, including a bottle of fizz, and she hoped they'd open it sooner rather than later.

"I think we need to take the next turning," he told her.

She nodded, leaning over the steering wheel to make sure she spotted it. Sure enough, a narrow lane appeared on her right. She signalled, despite there being no other cars on the road, and took the turning.

They followed the lane down. It grew even narrower, and she hoped they weren't going to meet any cars coming the other way.

"This feels like we've gone a lot further than a mile from the pub," she said, suddenly concerned about how remote they were. She glanced back down at her phone to see the single bar she'd previously had vanished. That niggle of worry reappeared inside her.

"You won't be turning down my offer of carrying you, then," he teased her.

She laughed but didn't really feel it. "No, I guess not."

"Look, there it is!"

Nestled in a small copse was the little cottage. It was single storey, with white stone walls and a red tiled roof. Rambling roses climbed across the front. There was a little patio with a round, iron table and chairs, with views across the rolling moorland.

Her heart immediately lifted. "Oh, it's beautiful."

Haiden grinned at her. "Told you."

She glanced down at the phone again to see the single bar had reappeared. "Does it have Wi-Fi?"

"No, it doesn't. We're supposed to be switching off from the outside world, Kristen. Remember?" That hard tone had come back to his voice. The last thing she wanted to do was upset him.

"Of course. Sorry."

"Maybe you should even leave your phone in the car," he suggested.

"I can't do that. What if something happens at home?"

"I'm sure Violet can deal with it."

But she shook her head. "No, I'm sorry, Haiden. I can't do that. Just because we're having a night together doesn't mean I'm no longer Ollie's mother." She glanced to his pockets. "What about your phone?"

"Oh, I left it at the house. I decided I didn't need it. I'd rather focus on us."

That had felt like a dig, but she let it slide. "It's just in case of emergencies."

"Of course."

They climbed out of the car, and she sucked in a lungful of sweet, clean air and immediately relaxed. "This is stunning."

"Yes, it is." He marched towards the front door. "Now, he said the key would be left out here somewhere."

"He just left a key?"

"Yeah, they don't get many passers-by to worry about out here."

"No, I guess not."

She stood back while Haiden set about lifting plant pots and peering under the mat. "Umm, didn't your friend tell you exactly where he'd left the key?"

"They rent this place out, and he said that people tend to leave the key in random places, even though they're instructed in where to put it when they leave."

"Oh, right." She laughed. "That must be a nightmare for them trying to figure out where people have left it each time."

"Yeah, it—" He cut off and stooped down to pluck something out from under a little statue of a hedgehog. "Got it."

"Well done. We'll have to put it somewhere else random when we leave," she joked.

He laughed and pulled her in for a kiss. "Come on, let's get inside."

He opened the door, and they stepped into the cottage together. The place was as beautiful on the inside as it was on the outside. The kitchen had natural wooden flooring and pale green painted units. Outside the windows were breathtaking views. She found the bedroom and smiled at the king-sized bed with white pillows and bedding. The whole place was light and airy, and her heart sang with happiness.

Haiden came up behind her, wrapping his arms around her waist. He planted a kiss on her neck, right behind her ear, sending little shivers of pleasure through her.

Her stomach, however, rumbled.

"I heard that," he growled against her earlobe.

She twisted in his arms. "I am hungry."

"Good thing I brought food, then. Go into the kitchen, and I'll bring the stuff in from the car. Have you got the keys?"

"Sure." She fished the car keys out of her pocket and handed them to him.

She got to work, opening the fridge and some of the cupboards, seeing what had been provided. Other than some bottles of tomato sauce and mayonnaise in the fridge, and some half empty spices in the cupboards, the place was bare. There was a small fire extinguisher in the corner. She guessed they were so far out, with such narrow roads, the owners figured they wouldn't be able to rely on a fire engine getting here quickly enough in case of a chip pan fire or something similar.

Haiden bustled back in, carrying a cooler. He opened it and produced a bottle of champagne.

"Oh, wow. I haven't had real champagne in years."

"Only the best for you," he said, tearing off the foil and popping the cork.

"If we drink too much of this, we won't be able to drive anywhere," she pointed out.

"That's okay. I don't think I want to go anywhere else, anyway. We have everything we need right here."

She took a sip of the champagne, bubbles going up her nose. Even from a couple of sips, she could already feel the alcohol going to her head. She didn't drink much, so even the smallest amount affected her, plus she was drinking on an empty stomach.

From the cool-box, Haiden pulled out baguettes, cold meats, salads, and cheeses, followed by chocolate cake—all her favourites. She found plates and knives. From a drawer, she plucked a serrated knife for the baguette, and a smaller, sharper one to slice the tomatoes and cucumber.

"Oh my God, this looks amazing," she said as she got to work slicing the salad, while Haiden cut the baguette into chunks. "You're really spoiling me."

"You deserve to be spoiled," he said, turning his gaze on her. His tone grew serious. "I mean it. After everything you've been through recently, it's important someone else takes care of you for a change."

Her face burned. "I don't do anything any other woman doesn't do."

"Yes, you do." He paused and then said, "I wanted to talk to you about something."

Her stomach twisted. She hoped this wasn't going to be bad news. It had all felt like it was going so well there for a moment. She should have known it wasn't going to last.

"I want you to know that I'll do anything to make you happy, Kristen. I think we have something really special here."

She gave him a smile. "So do I."

"I don't think you're really hearing me. I'm trying to tell you that I'll change my plans for you."

She frowned. "What are you talking about?"

"I know our relationship will make things difficult for you with the university housing, and I'm due to go back to Sweden after this semester. But what about if I didn't go? What about if I was no longer a part of the university either?"

Her mouth dropped open. "Are you talking about staying here? Quitting your master's degree, too?"

"Yes, if you want me to. I can move in with you as your boyfriend instead. And if I'm no longer studying, they can't complain about us being together."

"Wow. I mean... that's a big step. We haven't known each other for long."

"I know that, but when it's right, it's right. Don't you think?"

She didn't know what to think. He'd thrown this at her from out of nowhere. "I mean, I can see it being a solution, but it's still early days, and I wouldn't want you to give up your studies because of me. And what about your family?"

The family you haven't spoken to since you've been here.

He gave a half laugh. "I'm an adult, Kristen. I don't need to ask my family's permission to do something."

"No, of course not. But I still need to think about Ollie. Times have been hard lately, and I have to consider how this will affect him."

He huffed out a breath of exasperation. "Ollie is fine. You worry about him too much. It's not as though I'm not living there, anyway."

"But that's different. Ollie's never known me to be with anyone except for his dad."

He cocked an eyebrow. "The dad who's already married and has a child with someone else, you mean?"

She sighed. "Yes, I know it's double standards."

"You're allowed to have a life, too, Kristen. You're allowed to have a future."

"A future with you?"

"Why the hell not?"

She gestured towards him. "You're so young. You don't want to be tied down with some single mother."

He pursed his lips and shook his head. "That's not how I think of you."

"Maybe not, but that's how I have to think of myself. I can't just jump into a relationship without thinking things through, and I can't ignore the fact you're ten years younger than I am."

"Eight," he corrected.

"Okay, eight, and that you don't even live in this country. I can't build Ollie up to believing there's someone permanent in his life, only for that person to get bored and leave us."

His tone hardened again. "So, you're saying the only person who's standing between us is Ollie?"

She didn't like how that sounded at all, cool flickers of fear trickling down her spine.

"Let's change the subject," she said, turning her attention back to lunch, even though her appetite had all but vanished. The champagne had gone to her head, too, leaving her woozy.

She wanted to enjoy their time together, but instead she found herself to be anxious about the future.

She was aware of the weight of her phone in her pocket. She wanted to call home and check up on Ollie, but she knew Haiden would get shitty with her if she did. Her unease deepened. She shouldn't be with someone who was going to complain about her checking up on her son. He'd never been like that before, always more than happy to accommodate Ollie. Why the sudden change of heart?

Or was this normal? Would most men want her to set Ollie aside and focus on them instead? Were they naturally selfish creatures? She knew Stephen had been, but she certainly didn't want to tar everyone with the same brush. Perhaps she was obsessing about her home life too much. Haiden had gone to all this effort for her and had worn his heart on his sleeve, and she was the one making things difficult.

She forced a smile. "Let's eat, shall we? We could take it out on the patio so we can look at the view."

"Sure." He looked sullen, though, as though he was sulking, and a frisson of irritation shot through her.

She picked up her glass and took another swig of champagne, determined to have a good time. How had this all turned around so quickly? She put the salad and bread into a bowl and carried it outside so they could eat on the patio. Haiden followed with the hams and cheeses.

Kristen helped herself to a selection of food and chewed a piece of bread and cheese, though now her mouth was dry. There was a tension between them she didn't like, and she was suddenly aware of just how alone they were out here.

"Maybe we should walk down to the pub after we've eaten," she suggested lightly.

Haiden pursed his lips. "I don't know. It seems like a long way."

"Not too long." She suddenly wanted other people around. The silence between them had grown tense, and she was starting to regret coming out here.

"I'm just nipping to the loo." She got to her feet and leaned in to kiss him, hoping to lighten the mood between them, but he turned his face, so she just got his cheek.

Holding back tears, she went into the cottage and found the bathroom. She shut the door and locked it, and fished into her pocket for her phone. She longed to hear her son's voice.

Kristen pulled up the number for the house and tried that first, but there was no answer. Next, she tried Violet's phone, but again it just rang to answerphone. She considered leaving a message, but then decided not to. What could she say? That she missed them and wished she hadn't come? She didn't want to worry either her sister or her son.

What were they doing that they couldn't get to either phone? Her stomach knotted with worry. She hoped they were both safe. Maybe Stephen had taken a turn for the worse, and they'd had to rush to hospital. But surely Violet would have tried to call if something like that had happened.

Now she just had something else to worry about, and she couldn't even mention her concerns to Haiden. He'd complain about both her worrying, and that she'd called home in the first place when she was supposed to be concentrating on 'us.' Though she was no longer sure she wanted there to be an 'us.'

She was seeing a side to him that he'd kept well-hidden over the past few weeks.

Kristen got back to the table to discover Haiden had refilled her champagne glass.

"Cheers," he said, lifting his glass up in a toast.

She gave him a tight smile and picked hers up as well. They clinked glasses, but she didn't drink from hers. She already regretted having drunk as much as she had. It meant she wouldn't be able to just hop in the car and drive home if there was an emergency.

Haiden noticed and tilted his head towards her. "You know it's bad luck not to drink when someone toasts you."

"Oh, sorry." She took a sip. "I was miles away."

"Thinking about us, I hope," he teased, and she got a little flash of that old, relaxed, friendly Haiden.

"Of course."

He pulled her in and kissed her, and the kiss grew heated.

"Let's go to the bedroom," he murmured against her mouth.

Kristen pushed her negative thoughts away. She'd been overthinking things. They were here to enjoy each other.

She allowed him to tug her by the hand towards the bedroom. It wasn't as though she could say no, was it? Besides, the alcohol had loosened her reserves, and she wanted to feel good again. He was young and gorgeous, and really seemed to care about her. He wanted a future, and she was the one being difficult.

Chapter Twenty-nine

The late afternoon sun warmed strips across her naked body.

They'd had sex and then dozed for a while. It was starting to get late, the heat of the sun already diminishing.

"If we're going to go down to the pub, we should probably leave soon," she suggested, as she lay with her head rested on his bare chest. "It'll be dark coming back, otherwise."

He nuzzled his nose against the top of her head. "Is it bad that I want you all to myself?"

She looked up at him. "You mean you don't want to go for a walk?"

"Why do we need to, when we have everything we need right here?"

She still hadn't heard anything from Violet, and she wanted to slip away and try to call home again. She told herself it was good that she hadn't heard anything. It meant they were all happy and safe, didn't it? They didn't need her.

Or they were lying dead in a gutter?

Why did her mind always jump to the worst possibility?

"We don't need to go down to the pub," she suggested. "We could just take a walk down the lane. I spotted some wild ponies on the way up here. I'd love to go and see them."

He wriggled down in the bed, so he was facing her. "Why am I getting the feeling I'm not enough for you?" His tone was teasing, but there was something in his blue eyes—a hardness—that concerned her.

"Of course, you are." She placed her fingertips lightly to his cheek and leaned in to kiss him. His blond stubble grazed her skin. "But it seems a shame to let all this countryside go to waste, and I could do with stretching my legs before it gets dark."

"I guess we can have a romantic stroll."

She smiled with relief. "Great."

He climbed out of bed. As he unfolded his long legs and stretched out his lean back, she couldn't help but admire him. She needed to shake off this sense of foreboding. It was only being apart from Ollie that was causing this anxiety inside her. She was allowed for things to go well for once in her life. It wasn't healthy to keep looking into things so deeply. If you looked hard at anyone's relationship, she was sure you could pick things apart.

She washed up and dressed in something comfortable. Quickly, she shut the bathroom door and typed a quick text message to Violet asking her to call or message back that they were okay. It was stupid that she felt like she was doing something wrong, but she still slipped the phone into the back pocket of her jeans and pulled a baggy shirt over the top to hide it.

"Ready?" Haiden called out to her.

"Ready!"

Together, they left the cottage and took the path up towards the road and the moorland beyond. Haiden swung his arm around her shoulders as they strolled, chatting comfortably. Soon enough, they came across a small group of the wild ponies she'd spotted in the car.

"Oh, look," she exclaimed. "There's a baby foal. How sweet."

"Yeah, sweet," he agreed, though she had the feeling she was boring him.

They walked a little farther and stopped at an overlook to take in the view. While Haiden was distracted, she checked her phone. The one bar coverage was down to nothing now.

"We should probably head back," she said. "It'll be dark soon."

Haiden gave her a strange look. "Not afraid of the dark, are you?"

"Not normally." And that was the truth, but out here, with nothing else around, the idea of it getting dark sent a wriggle of fear down her spine. But they'd be tucked up in the cosy cottage, maybe snuggled under a blanket on the couch, getting to know each other better.

"Come on, then." He caught up her hand in his. "Let's get back. I'd rather be at the cottage with you, anyway." And he pulled her in for a kiss.

It only took them half an hour to get back to the cottage, but by that time the temperature had noticeably dropped, and the skyline was awash in pinks and purples, like a watercolour painting. They hadn't locked the door when they'd left, and they tumbled back into the cottage, rubbing their arms and stamping feet.

"I'm glad we didn't eat everything at lunchtime," she commented, noticing how they'd left everything out on the worktops. "It's going to have to be dinner as well."

So much for the cosy pub meal.

He smirked. "Well, we did work up an appetite."

Kristen deliberately misunderstood him. "Yes, we must have walked a couple of miles at least."

Her phone buzzed in her back pocket.

She pulled out the phone. There was only one bar, but it was enough to receive calls. Violet's name flashed up on screen and she breathed a sigh of relief.

"It's my sister."

His frown deepened. "Leave it."

"No, I can't. Ollie might need me."

She swiped to answer and took a few steps away from Haiden.

"Hi! I've been trying to get hold of you guys. Everything okay at home?"

Violet's voice came down the line. "You sound strange. Are you on speaker phone?"

She wasn't the only one whose voice sounded strange. Violet's was strangled, high pitched as though she was frightened of something. Her heart lurched. Had her instincts been right? "Is everything okay with Ollie?"

"Yes, he's fine. Are you on speakerphone, Kristen?"

Kristen frowned. Why was she so insistent on her answering that question? "No, I'm not. It's just the reception around here is terrible. I only have one bar."

"I need to pass you over to someone, but just pretend you're still talking to me, okay? It's really important, Kristen."

"What? What are you—"

But a male voice cut in. "Ms Scott, this is Detective Superintendent Craig Miles. I'm head of Major Crime, and Serious and Organised Crime for this area."

Alarm spiked through her. "Sorry?"

"Ms Scott, are you with Haiden Lindgren right now?"

She lifted her gaze to where Haiden was watching her intently, his eyebrows arched as though silently asking her what was being said. "Yes, I am."

"Ms Scott, I need you to listen to me very carefully, but whatever you do, don't have a reaction to what I'm telling you. Speak calmly, and don't do anything rash. If you can, reply only in yes or no answers, okay?"

Worry trickled through her, and her gaze flicked back to Haiden and then away again. She didn't know what this was all about, but to hide her reaction to whatever she was about to be told, she angled her body away from Haiden and ducked her head. "Okay, I understand."

"You're not safe right now."

"What?"

"The body of Haiden Lindgren has been discovered in a forest just outside of Kalmar in Sweden."

"I'm sorry... What?" Her mind blurred. What the hell was he talking about? Haiden was standing right there. "I don't understand."

"The man you're currently with is not Haiden Lindberg. We believe his name is Filip Nilsson, and we believe he had reason to murder Haiden Lindberg and pose in his place."

The world turned in a slow, dizzying circle. Her vision went black at the edges, tunnelling. Her stomach dropped, her pulse thundering in her ears. A rush of cold swept over her body, quickly replaced by a flood of heat.

"That... that isn't possible." She didn't want to believe it. This was crazy. She'd been living with this man for the past month. He'd told her everything about himself. She'd allowed him into her home, into her body. He'd played with her son, and they'd talked of a future. Surely, this couldn't be true. It must be some kind of sick joke.

She wanted to turn to Haiden and demand for him to tell her the truth, to beg him to tell her this was crazy and a total lie. She wanted to pretend none of the last few minutes had happened.

Though she didn't want to believe what the police officer was telling her, something rang true. Certain things had never quite pieced together. How he'd been avoiding contact with any family back home. How he'd never had any friends and had been so willing to give up a course he clearly wouldn't have known anything about.

"Your sister said you're staying up in a cottage on the moors. Are you able to give me your current address?"

She wracked her brains, trying to figure out if she knew it. But she didn't think Haiden had ever told her, and she hadn't been paying that much attention to the names of the little areas when they'd been driving through.

"No, I'm sorry. I can't."

"Okay, don't worry. We can find you. Is there anyone else with you right now, other than him? Yes or no answers, remember."

"No."

"Is there someplace safe you can go where there will be other people?"

She thought to the pub. She opened her mouth to tell him that and then remembered what he'd said about yes or no answers. "Yes, there is."

"Good. I want you to try to get there. We're working on getting a warrant to triangulate the position of your phone. If you can just slip it into your pocket to make sure it's on you all the time, that would be helpful. Do you understand?"

She tried to make her voice bright. "Yes, no problem."

"You can even leave this line open, if you want. We'll keep someone on the other end."

"I'm not sure my battery's going to last," she said, trying to sound chirpy. "I need to charge it."

"No problem. Just make sure you keep it on."

She felt detached from reality, as though she'd woken up in a nightmare. Surely this wasn't happening. They must have made a mistake.

She wanted to ask if her sister and Ollie were all right, but she was mindful of the yes or no part. Haiden, or whatever the fuck his name was, was watching her intensely. She could feel his gaze burning into the back of her neck. Nausea swirled inside her at the possibility he was a murderer. She'd had sex with this man. She'd been more intimate with him than with anyone else for years, and he'd turned out to be a killer.

She gulped back a sob, knowing she couldn't let him know what she knew. She had to pretend like everything was just as it had been.

"We're sending someone out to you, Ms Scott. Just hang in there. Both the mountain rescue and the police will be with you soon."

"Okay."

She swiped the phone to end the call and slipped it back into her pocket. Swallowing hard, she did her best to compose herself, but she was rooted to the spot. A high-pitched buzzing filled her ears, and she fought against the bile rising up the back of her throat. Haiden wasn't Haiden. His name was Filip Nilsson. He was some random man who'd murdered the real Haiden and taken his place. Oh, God. She'd slept with him. She'd kissed him and let him be around her son.

She was breathing hard now, her head swimming. She wanted to bend over and put her hands on her knees and try to get control of herself again, but she knew she'd look too obvious. She remembered what the police officer had told her about remaining calm.

How was she going to get to the pub without him wanting to come with her? She should be okay to drive by now—hours had passed since she'd drunk the champagne. Maybe she should just grab the keys and make a run for it? But if she gave him any idea that the police were on to him, he'd run, too. She needed for them to arrest him so she'd at least have the knowledge he was behind bars. If he got away, what was to say he wouldn't come back for her, or, even worse, try to get to Ollie? If he was capable of murdering once, who knew if he'd do it again.

Kristen sucked in a long breath, pasted a smile on her face, and turned towards him.

He studied her with concern. "Everything okay?"

"Yes, fine."

"Is Violet coping with Ollie?"

She pulled a face. "Not really. Ollie is upset and missing me. I'm not really sure I should be staying."

His tone hardened. "We're not running back home just because Ollie's being a brat."

Despite everything, she bristled at the insult of her son. "He's not a brat!"

He put out his hand. "Give me the phone."

Her blood ran cold. "What?"

"You heard me. Every time you've thought about home or had contact with home since we left has ended up with things being weird between us."

She balled her fists, aware she was trembling, and not wanting him to notice. "That's not my fault. You're making me feel like I'm doing the wrong thing by caring about my son." She could barely believe she was even having this conversation. None of that even mattered. He wasn't who he said he was. He was a killer. She struggled to get her head around it.

He took a step closer, and inadvertently, she stepped back.

Right away, she knew she'd done the wrong thing. A muscle in his jaw twitched and his hands clenched and unclenched.

His tone lowered, smooth and cold. "Who was really on the phone?"

Her heart fluttered like a trapped moth in her chest. "I told you, it was my sister. She was worried about Ollie."

"So, she let you talk to him? You got to say goodnight."

"Yes, of course I did."

He gave a cold laugh. "Don't bullshit me, Kristen. I know you didn't talk to Ollie."

"How could you possibly know that?"

"Because your voice changes when you talk to him. It goes higher, and is softer, and you call him baby or sweetheart. You don't talk to him in the way you were talking just then."

Fuck.

"Who was on the phone really?"

"It was my sister, I promise." She was desperate for him to believe her.

"Let me see the phone, then?"

She couldn't give it to him. If she did, he was bound to not give it back. What if he destroyed the phone, and the police weren't able to track her position? Would he kill her, too?

His eyes narrowed. "You know, don't you?"

"Know what?" she tried to bluff.

"Who I really am."

Oh God.

Her gaze darted past him, towards the front door. Could she make it? Just run. It wasn't what she was supposed to do, and yes, maybe he'd run as well, and the police would lose track of him, but this was her life on the line.

He widened his stance, clearly reading what was on her mind. "Don't even think about it."

"Please, Haiden… or whatever your name is. I have a son. He needs me."

"Oh, I *know* you have a son. Isn't that all I hear about!" He jabbed a finger out towards her. "And don't try to pretend like I haven't helped you, Kristen. You and Ollie. I've done everything I can to make you happy."

"What are you talking about?" Her confusion deepened.

"It's because of me that Felix no longer goes to the school and Ollie's been able to return. You should be thanking me!"

She stepped back in shock. "What? Felix was in an accident. A horrible accident."

He sighed and shook his head. "Yes, it was horrible. But things had to be done. You said yourself, no one was doing anything to help Ollie."

She stared in horror. "What did you do?"

He didn't answer her, only pressed his lips together and glanced away.

"What did you do?" Her voice rose to a high-pitched shriek. "What did you *do*?"

"Only what needed to be done. A little shove from behind when he'd been up in his treehouse. He hadn't even seen me coming."

"Felix is just a little boy!"

"A little boy who would have grown into a violent man, if something hadn't been done. You wanted to hurt him yourself, Kristen. You told me as much."

"I threatened it in the heat of an argument. That was all! I'd never have actually wanted any harm to come to him."

"Oh, be real. Don't kid yourself that you didn't feel that violence coursing through your veins when you saw what he'd done to Ollie. Don't tell me that you weren't relieved to your very core when you heard he wasn't coming back to school."

"No, no." She shook her head, hating that every word coming out of his mouth was the truth. She *had* wanted Felix to hurt. She *had* been relieved when she'd found out he wasn't coming back to school any time soon.

"I did it for you, Kristen. I did *everything* for you."

"Everything?" Her mind raced to figure out what else he was talking about. "Stephen?"

"Now, that one I actually enjoyed. Shame I didn't kill the son of a bitch, but you know he had it coming."

She shook her head, backing away. "No, stop."

He moved closer. "I want you to know I didn't plan any of this, Kristen. I mean, obviously I planned part of it—the start where I killed the real Haiden. I needed to get out of the country, and what better way than by posing as someone else? No one ever really looks at the passport photographs of everyone on those big coaches, and I looked enough like the real Haiden to not get questioned—tall, with blond hair and blue eyes. It was enough to flash them the photograph in his passport, and they just moved on. It was laughably easy, really."

"Why did you choose me?"

"Just a happy coincidence. I had originally been planning on pulling a vanishing act shortly after I arrived, but then I saw you at the coach station, and everything changed. I meant everything I said about that first time I saw you. I know it's a cliché, but it was like a thunderbolt hitting me in the chest. And then you were so kind to me, welcoming me into your family like I was a part of it. I never really had a family of my own. Not a decent one, anyway. My mother ran off when I was small, and left me with an alcoholic, abusive father, and you can see how that turned out."

Her mouth gaped. "You've killed people."

"Yes, well, I was hoping you'd never have to find that out. It was stupid of me, really. I should have left a long time ago, but instead, we kept getting closer and closer, and I just couldn't bring myself to leave."

"You hurt Felix. And Stephen..."

He snatched up her hand, his grip like a vice, and she stifled a scream. "I did all those things for *you*, Kristen. Can't you see that? It made me so fucking angry to sit back and watch how people were treating you. You have literally lived your life for everyone else—taking care of Ollie, and your sister, and putting up with that arsehole ex-husband treating you like shit. Someone had to do something."

She shook her head, hardly able to believe what she was hearing. Her entire body vibrated with adrenaline. "All those things that were happening... the broken plant pots and the window, and the car tyres. Was that you? Were you trying to frighten me?"

"Fuck, no! Haven't you listened to a single word I've said?" His eyes darkened with anger and she tried to backpedal.

"No, of course, it wasn't you. I'm sorry." Her voice stammered and shook as she spoke. "The police are on their way, Haiden." Shit, that wasn't even his name. "I mean Filip. You might as well just let me go."

"No, I can't. Not now. I've told you everything."

"The police know everything anyway."

He shook his head. "They don't. They don't know about Felix or Stephen."

"I won't tell them, I swear."

He snorted. "You expect me to believe that?"

"Yes, believe it. I swear I won't say a word. Just walk out of here now and keep going."

He wrinkled his nose. "I can't do that."

"What are you going to do to me?"

He didn't answer her question but moved closer. "I could have loved you, Kristen. That's the saddest thing about all of this. What we had was real."

She shook her head. "No, it wasn't. I don't even know who you are."

She had to buy herself some time. The police were coming, but the only thing they had to track her location was the mobile phone in her back pocket. She remembered how she'd asked if he was taking his phone with him, and he'd said he was leaving it back at the house. Was that how the police had found him? No, they wouldn't have even needed to do that. Once they'd realised the real Haiden was dead, they must have figured out the killer was posing as Haiden and tracked him down to her house. If only they hadn't chosen this weekend to go away. Had he known they were closing in on him? But it was better that they were away. If they'd been at the house, Ollie would have got caught up in all of this.

Inwardly, she groaned at the thought of all the police turning up at her house. They'd probably searched it. The neighbours would all be talking, and poor Ollie and Violet would have been confused and terrified.

His broad form blocked the way. She'd never get past him to the car.

Shit. Where were the car keys, anyway? She remembered throwing them to him when he'd gone back out to the vehicle to bring in the bags. He must still have them on him. She'd never get away by just running. He was taller and younger and would catch her in an instant. But without the car keys, what choice did she have?

"You need to give me that phone, Kristen," he said, taking another step towards her.

She couldn't let him get the phone. If he took it and destroyed it, the police might never find her.

"No."

"Give. Me. The. Phone."

She might not be able to get past him, but there were other options.

"Now, Kristen!"

He lunged for her.

Chapter Thirty

With a scream, she spun on her heels and threw herself towards the hallway. Expecting to feel his hand clamping onto her shoulder or around her throat at any second, she could barely believe it when she slammed her way into the bathroom and managed to get the door shut behind her. Frantic, dizzy with adrenaline, and her hands shaking, she fiddled with the lock.

He crashed into the door from the other side. The door bowed, but she managed to crack the lock into place. She fell back, panting hard. The backs of her legs hit the side of the bathtub, and the strength went out of her limbs. She sank down onto the edge, staring at the locked door in terror.

His voice boomed from the other side. "Open the door, Kristen! I mean it."

She didn't answer.

Desperate, she looked around, trying to figure out her next move. There was a window, but only the narrow top part opened, and even then by only a few inches, and she knew there was no possibility of her squeezing through it.

A crash came at the door, and she jumped, her heart pounding.

"I'll break the fucking door down!" he bellowed.

Thank God for old, heavy doors. If she was in a new build right now, he'd have broken through within a minute. The bangs came again, the sound of his shoulder hitting the door. The door rattled in the frame, but it didn't give, and somehow the lock held, too.

She sat, staring, her gaze dropping down to the substantial gap between the bottom of the door and the floor, watching the shadow his body created. Her entire body shook violently. She needed to do something with the phone. The moment he got in here, he would try and take it off her. But if he couldn't find it, it would buy her more time.

Where could she hide it?

The room wasn't big, and there weren't many places to hide things—the small bathroom cabinet, a rack filled with towels, behind the toilet, perhaps?

She glanced back to the window. Could she risk throwing the phone out, into the garden? What if it broke, and the battery fell out? Plus, the screen was already cracked, and another fall might break it completely. But would that make it untraceable? She wished she knew more about this kind of thing.

She looked back around the bathroom. She could hide the phone in the toilet cistern, perhaps? But would it get wet?

Indecision rendered her useless.

The banging against the door had stopped. Where had he gone? Shit. Would he come around the side of the house and smash the window instead? If he did, she'd know the door was free and she'd be able to get out that way.

Unease trickled through her. What was Haiden—no, not Haiden, Filip—playing at?

The shadow appeared beneath the door once more, and she braced herself for another slam of his body against the wood. But instead, something black and rubbery was pushed under the door. A hose? She narrowed her eyes, wondering what was happening. Whatever it was, she was sure it wouldn't be anything good.

From the other side of the door, a loud hissing started, and suddenly white foaming powder exploded from the black rubber nozzle and filled the small bathroom.

Kristen staggered backwards, her lungs trying to suck in oxygen, but only inhaling white powder. The identity of the rubber thing suddenly came to her. He'd taken the fire extinguisher from the kitchen. The son of a bitch was trying to gas her out.

Another blast from the fire extinguisher filled the room, and her lungs tightened. She coughed, her hand clutched to her mouth. Instinctively, she clambered towards the window, but the tiny gap wasn't enough to replace the amount of oxygen the chemicals in the room were displacing.

"I'll keep it coming, Kristen," he bellowed. "I won't stop. I'll force you out of there. Open the door, or you'll die locked in a bathroom."

"Then I'll die!" She wanted to sound brave, but her voice was weak and strangled.

More CO_2 filled the room.

Coughing, her hand half-covering her mouth and nose, she knew she had to make a decision. He was going to tear through this small bathroom in a matter of minutes, and then he'd find the phone. She needed to buy herself time.

Shit shit shit.

With tears streaming down her face, she grabbed a towel and went back to the window. It was already open a crack—probably the only thing saving her lungs right now—and she pushed it open as far as it would go. Then she wrapped the phone up in the towel and held it out of the window.

Please don't break, please don't break, please don't break.

And she let it drop.

It hit the ground on the outside of the cottage, and she winced, but couldn't do anything now. She just had to hope it was still in one piece. At least now, to get the phone when he realised what she'd done with it, he'd be forced to leave the cottage to go and get it. Hoping it would confuse him, she yanked the window shut again, and gave in to the coughing. Another blast of CO_2 came from the fire extinguisher, and she felt like her throat was closing over. She was struggling to breathe.

"Okay, okay. I'm unlocking the door." Her vision blurred from tears caused by all the coughing and also the chemicals in the room.

She didn't have any choice. If she kept it locked, she'd die in here. By the time the police showed up, he'd be long gone, and all they'd find was her body. All she could think about was Ollie and how he'd cope without her. Violet would step in to take care of him, especially with Stephen in hospital, too, but it wouldn't be the same. He needed his mum, and she couldn't let this psychopath take that from him.

Her chest tightened, her lungs contracting. Her vision started to pull away from the edges. Was she going to pass out? No, she couldn't. If she did, she'd be dead.

Kristen clawed at the door, unable to bring the lock into focus. Her fingers caught cool metal and then slipped from it again. The room turned in a slow circle, and for a moment she forgot where she was and what she was supposed to be doing.

No, no, no.

She grappled for the lock again, and her fingers found purchase. To her relief, it clicked open. In her desperation for air, she'd forgotten the man on the other side.

The door burst inward, and she staggered back.

He was on her in an instant. Grabbing the front of her shirt, he swung her around and shoved her out of the bathroom. He didn't let go of her, though, matching her movements with his own, so he remained towering over her.

His hands wrapped around her throat. "Where is it, Kristen? What did you do with the fucking phone?"

She clamped her mouth shut, determined not to tell him, no matter what he did to her.

Sensing she wasn't going to tell him, he gave a roar of frustration and pulled back his fist. His knuckles met with her cheekbone, rocking her head backwards, pain blasting like a firework across her cheek.

He threw her to the floor, and she landed on her back, hitting her head and what little air she'd managed to inhale bursting from her lungs. Everything seemed to hurt now, so she struggled to distinguish one pain from another.

Then he was on top of her. "Tell me!"

Her eyes rolled, and she fought to stay in control of her body. The weakness and disorientation must have been caused by the powder she'd inhaled.

He gave another roar and grabbed her by the sides of her face and lifted her head up before slamming it back against the wooden floorboards.

The world tunnelled. She was barely aware of him getting off her again and going back into the bathroom. She heard the crashes as he was throwing things around. Just as she'd expected, he tore everything apart, swiping toiletries off the side, so they fell into the sink with a clatter.

With him distracted, she managed to crawl onto all fours. Her head swam with dizziness, but she knew she needed to get out of there. She winced as a loud crack came from behind her, signalling the bath panel being torn off. He was literally pulling the place apart to find the phone. Soon enough, he'd realise it wasn't in there, and that there was only one other place it could be.

Had enough time passed yet for the police to have traced the phone? It felt like both a matter of brief moments, and the longest time of her life since she'd spoken to the officer. But if they hadn't yet traced it, and he got outside and destroyed the mobile, all hope would be lost.

Kristen staggered to her feet. He was still engrossed in trying to find the phone, and either hadn't noticed her trying to run, or figured there was nowhere she could go. He still had the car keys, and there was only open moorland around them. Even if she ran, he'd catch her within minutes.

She spotted the board where they'd prepared lunch. The bread knife, and the smaller knife she'd used to slice tomatoes and cucumber, were still there.

"Kristen!" His roar came from behind her. "Give me that fucking phone!"

Throwing herself forward, she snatched up the bread knife. Then she picked up the smaller of the two, weighing up which would be better.

"You're not getting away that easily!"

She spun around, brandishing the bigger of the knives. "Stay away from me."

"You're going to cut me?" He no longer looked like the Haiden she'd known. Something had changed about him, his features harder, his eyes as cool and pale as glacial ice. This was the killer she'd brought into her home.

She stabbed the knife in his direction, fighting against another round of coughing that tickled the back of her throat. "Stay back!"

He darted for her, jabbing out with his hand. She screamed and slashed with the knife. She missed.

He laughed, his ice blue eyes flashing with anger. "What do you think you're doing, Kristen? You're not going to hurt me. We're lovers, remember?"

"You're crazy."

The knife trembled in her grip. She wanted to look strong, but she was fighting against the crap she'd inhaled from the fire extinguisher, and the bang to the head he'd given her. He was so big, swamping the space in front of her, alive and filled with cold determination. He was going to kill her.

She lunged for him again, swiping the knife down in an arc. He lifted his hand to bat her away but misjudged the speed she was moving, and she caught his forearm. He yelled and yanked away, and she saw a slash of red. Brazened by the small win, she attacked again, going for his face this time. The knife sliced down his cheek, and a flap of skin peeled away.

Kristen screamed in wild triumph.

He was furious. "You bitch!"

Lowering his shoulder, he rushed her. It was like being hit by a bull, sending her flying. She lost her grip on the knife as she fell, slamming to the ground. The air exploded from her lungs, leaving her gasping. Sharp pain stabbed into her hip, but she ignored the wound and the feel of hot wetness soaking her jeans.

The man she'd known as Haiden was on top of her again, his bodyweight pinning her down. One hand clamped down on her throat, strangling her, while the other reached out to where the knife had fallen.

Her gaze darted wildly to the bread knife. His fingertips scraped the handle. Almost there. He reached out farther, stretching as far as he could without removing his weight from her torso, or his hand from her throat.

He got his fingers around the handle of the breadknife, more focused on that than what she was doing. As he lifted it high, ready to drive it into her chest, she reached to her hip. With a strangled scream, she yanked out the smaller knife she'd hidden when she'd picked up the breadknife and swung her arm. The small but sharp blade sank into the side of his neck.

His whole body went rigid. His eyes widened in shock, and his mouth dropped open. He tried to suck in a breath, but there was only a strange whistling sound, and a red bubble of blood appeared between his lips. The bread knife fell from his fingers and clattered to the floor.

Kristen used what remained of her strength and shoved him off her. He fell onto his back and lay there, gasping, his fingers hovering around the hilt of the knife protruding from his neck. His hand wrapped around it, and he pulled. The blade slid out of his flesh, but with it came an arc of blood. The flap in his cheek, combined with the hole in his throat was a nightmare brought to life.

She dragged herself backwards on the floor, not daring to take her eyes off him in case he came after her again.

But more blood gurgled from his lips, and finally the light in his eyes faded.

Chapter Thirty-one

S he didn't know how long she'd been sitting on the kitchen floor. She was barely aware of her surroundings, preferring to withdraw inside her head and block out the scene in front of her. All her limbs were freezing, and she couldn't remember anything beyond the knife going into the neck of the man she'd believed to be Haiden Lindgren, but who was actually a stranger called Filip Nilsson.

Outside, the familiar hum of car engines approached, punctuated by the slamming of car doors. Still, she remained in the exact same position.

Movement came in the doorway. She recognised the uniform of police officers. Perhaps she should have been relieved to see them, but she felt nothing. Only cold and detached.

"Ms Scott?"

"He's dead," she called out, her voice trembling.

One of the police officers stepped more fully into the room, spotting the body. "Shit." Then he called out, "In here!"

Was she going to be arrested for murder? She'd killed him. In that moment, she'd *wanted* him dead. Haiden—no, Filip—had been right when he'd said she had that capacity for violence inside her.

"Ms Scott? Are you all right?" The police officer came and crouched beside her. "Are you hurt?"

She shook her head, not trusting herself to speak.

"You're bleeding." He gestured to her leg.

Dumbly, she glanced down at her thigh to discover her jeans were dark and wet. Of course, she'd stabbed herself accidentally when he'd thrown her to the floor. She'd completely forgotten. Was that why she was so cold? A volley of coughing clutched at her lungs and she spluttered and hacked until her eyes streamed.

"We need a paramedic in here," he called out. "And we're going to need the coroner's office, too."

She was only vaguely aware of more people entering the room. An older man in a suit approached her. "Ms Scott. I'm Detective Superintendent Miles. We spoke on the phone."

"If I go to prison," she said, her voice not sounding as though it belonged to her, "will you make sure my sister looks after my son?"

"You won't be going to prison. There will be an enquiry, of course, but we know what kind of man Filip Nilsson is. Was. He's wanted for three other deaths in Sweden. We can see this was clearly self-defence."

Three other deaths? Deaths that didn't include the real Haiden.

He touched her arm, trying to be reassuring, but she jerked away.

"Don't worry about any of that now," he said. "We're going to take you to the local hospital and get you checked over. There'll be plenty of time to go through the events leading up to now when you're doing better."

She nodded and allowed him to help her to her feet. She struggled to put weight on her bad leg, but he supported her.

As they moved at a slow lurch through the cottage, she couldn't tear her eyes from the body.

The man she'd killed.

The cold she'd been experiencing went right down to her soul. She was responsible for a man's death. The life she'd been living for the past month had been a lie. She'd had a murderer in her home, living under the same roof as her son.

Kristen lowered her head and barked out a sob.

He'd hurt Felix, and Stephen, too. She'd brought this man into their lives. What could have happened if the police hadn't discovered who he really was? Who would have been next? Would he have set his sights on Violet, or even Ollie? She couldn't stand the thought of it.

She went over the things he'd said before he'd died. Had he truly believed he was helping her by harming Felix and Stephen?

No, he had a twisted mind. He just used her as an excuse to hurt people.

"This wasn't your fault," Detective Superintendent Miles told her, as though reading her thoughts. "You were in the wrong place at the wrong time. You could have been anyone."

Her heart twisted. Was that supposed to make her feel better? She'd finally found a man she'd believed she might even be able to love again, and it turned out that he was a murderer, and not only that, she could have been anyone? Was it better or worse to think that there may have been the tiniest amount of truth in their relationship? That some of it may have been real.

Her head hurt trying to think about it.

They stepped outside. It was fully dark now, and the fresh, cool air went some way to bringing her out of her stupor. She suddenly realised how much her leg hurt and how tight her chest was.

She remembered something. "My phone. I threw it out of the bathroom window."

He nodded. "We've got it. I'm afraid it's going to need to be used as evidence."

She hadn't thought of that. "What about my family?"

"They're being kept informed about you. We'll let them know what hospital you're being taken to, and they can meet you there."

As though he'd conjured up the vehicle, the lights of an ambulance rumbled down the little lane towards the cottage. It pulled to a halt, and two paramedics jumped out and ran to her.

"We'll talk again later," the inspector said, before patting her on the arm and vanishing back inside the cottage.

SHE WAS TAKEN TO HOSPITAL to be treated for concussion, shock, and the inhalation of the powder from the fire extinguisher.

"Mummy!"

Ollie ran into the room, shortly followed by Violet.

Kristen pushed herself to sitting in the hospital bed, trying not to wince at her now bandaged leg. She'd needed stitches, but otherwise she'd escaped relatively unharmed. She'd been very lucky. Tears filled her eyes at the sight of her family, and she put her arms out for Ollie to clamber into.

"Be careful of your mum," Violet warned.

"No, it's fine," she said, hugging Ollie tight, pressing her nose into his soft hair and inhaling the scent of him. Was there any smell in the world that was better? "I don't know what I would have done if something happened to you. I love you so much, and I totally take you for granted. I'm so sorry."

"It's okay," Violet said. "None of this is your fault."

Kristen wished she could believe her. Silent tears streamed down her face, dampening Ollie's hair.

"He tricked everyone, Kristen." Her sister took her hand to offer her some comfort. "It wasn't just you. It was everyone he met. Shit, even I thought he was a good guy."

"Aunty Vi!" Ollie scolded. "You used a swear word."

Kristen exchanged a teary smile with Violet, knowing that what had happened deserved more than just one swear word.

Kristen shook her head. "I'm still struggling to believe this isn't all one bad dream. How did I not know who he was?"

"The university messed up, big time. And so did the authorities when they didn't check his passport properly. This isn't your fault."

She sniffed and nodded. "I know."

But even though she knew what her sister was saying was the truth, she still couldn't get her head around it. She'd cared about a man who'd been dead in an unmarked grave for the past month. No, it hadn't been him she'd cared about. It had been the Haiden that Filip Nilsson had created.

A forgery. A ghost. A shadow.

Her Haiden had never existed.

Chapter Thirty-two

"Are you ready?" Violet asked Kristen.

Kristen squeezed her hand and nodded. "I think so."

"You don't think this is a bit weird?"

She shrugged. "I don't know, maybe, but it feels like closure."

She was about to meet Mr and Mrs Lindgren at the spot where the real Haiden's body had been discovered. One of the hardest parts of her recovery over the past couple of months had been mentally trying not to think of Haiden as Haiden. The man who she'd killed at the cottage had been called Filip, and yet she couldn't shake the idea that it wasn't Filip who had been killed, but the Haiden he'd been impersonating. She struggled with nightmares in which the Haiden she'd known was still alive and was coming back for her. Even though she'd seen his body, the idea that there had been two of them made it impossible for her to move on.

Haiden Lindgren's parents had struggled, too, understandably. They'd believed their son to be alive for a month after he'd been so brutally murdered and left in a shallow grave. They wanted to meet the woman who'd lived with the man who'd killed their son and offered to cover the costs to bring both Kristen and Violet out to Sweden for the weekend.

"I'm not sure this is such a good idea," Violet admitted.

"I have to do it. It's the only thing I can think to do that will help me move on."

Violet squeezed her hand in return. "I hope it does, Kristen. You deserve some peace."

"Thanks, Sis."

One good thing that had come out of all of this was that her relationship with Violet had been greatly improved. Violet admitted how frightened she'd been, thinking she was going to lose her, and she realised how important her sister and nephew were, and that she'd make more of an effort. She even moved in with Kristen, paying the rent so Kristen wasn't short on the income. Violet knew that while Kristen needed the money, she also didn't want to be the only adult alone in the house right now, and she wasn't about to bring another stranger into her home any time soon.

Kristen had left Ollie with Stephen and Lisa for the weekend while she and Violet flew out to Sweden. She wouldn't have wanted Ollie to be in this situation. It had all been confusing enough for the poor kid. Stephen was home and doing better. He still had a noticeable slur, but physically he was almost back to his old self. During his recovery, Kristen had got much friendlier with Lisa, and had even confessed to her fear that Stephen had wanted to take Ollie from her before the accident.

Lisa had reacted with horror. "No offence to Ollie, Kristen, because he's as sweet as a five-year-old boy can be, but the idea of having three kids under the age of six at home full time would be way too much for me to handle."

Kristen had managed a laugh at that. Lisa was a good woman—better than Stephen deserved, not that he'd ever realise that.

An enquiry into exactly what had happened to allow Filip Nilsson to pose as Haiden Lindgren for so long had been conducted. It involved a proper investigation into who was responsible for the window breaking and tyre slashing that had occurred while Filip had been a resident at Kristen's house. It turned out one of their neighbours had security cameras which caught the outside of Kristen's house, and had therefore captured the person who'd been destroying her property.

Rachelle Hurst had eventually admitted that she'd been the one trying to scare Kristen, hoping she could frighten her into leaving the area. She was only charged with a misdemeanour and ordered to pay damages, but she was also struck off the parent teachers association, and there wouldn't be much chance of seeing her up at the school again—something Kristen was particularly relieved about now that she was back at work. Felix himself was doing better. Young bodies healed well, it turned out, and he'd made surprising advances in regaining feeling in his legs. Of course, they wouldn't be staying local now. Even with Felix on the mend, everyone knew what Rachelle had done, revealing herself for the absolute bitch she really was, and they'd be moving out of the area.

The owner of the cottage where it had all come to a head also spoke to the police. It seemed Haiden, or Filip, as he now needed to be known, had overheard a conversation the owner had had with an actual friend, offering up the place, and had decided to take it on himself to plan the weekend there. The owner had since had the locks changed and promised to increase the security at the cottage. She imagined he'd probably be doing some redecorating, too. It was hard enough being at her house, knowing that Filip had touched everything, without having to imagine his dead body and the blood splatter every time she went into the kitchen.

Kristen pulled her thoughts from the investigation and focused on the place the events of the past few months had brought her.

The spot marking the real Haiden Lindberg's original shallow grave—the place where his body had lain for almost a month—was marked by a small cross and some flowers. They'd walked through the forest of spruce and pine trees, about half a mile from the road, before they'd found it. Of course, Haiden Lindgren's body was no longer here. It had been taken for forensics back when it had first been discovered.

Violet nudged her in the side. "They're here."

The shape of two figures made their way through the trees.

Kristen sucked in a lungful of air, steadying her nerves. How would they feel about her? Did they think she was a terrible person for having a relationship with the man she'd believed to have been their son? Filip had killed Haiden before she'd even known he existed, so she couldn't be held responsible for that part, but perhaps they felt she should have picked up there being something wrong sooner? Nothing she could have done would have saved the real Haiden, though.

She looked up as the couple in their sixties approached, the woman with her arm hooked through the man's.

The couple noticed the two other women standing there, and both gave a tight smile and a nod. Kristen couldn't imagine how they were feeling. She'd come here for herself, but she suddenly put herself in their position. How would she cope if this was Ollie's grave she was standing by now? It didn't matter how old your children got; they were always your children.

The new arrivals stopped on the other side of the shallow grave. "Kristen?" the man said, looking between them.

Kristen nodded and leaned forward to shake his hand. "Mr Lindgren. I'm sorry we're meeting in these circumstances."

"It's Hugo, please. This is my wife, Brigetta."

Both of the real Haiden's parents were blond with blue eyes. Yes, Filip could have easily passed as their son. And, like Filip, their English was perfect and barely held an accent.

"This is my sister Violet. I'm so sorry for what happened to your son." She found herself blinking back tears. How would things have been if it had been the real Haiden who'd come to live with her? Of course, she didn't expect for things to have been anything like they'd been with Filip, but maybe they'd have been friends.

"Thank you," Brigetta said. "And thank you for avenging the death of our boy."

It felt strange how she felt like she knew their son, even though she'd never met him. It hadn't been their Haiden she'd known.

"We couldn't believe it when we found out that bastard had been pretending to be our son all that time," Hugo continued. "Walking around, using his name. It's like he was dancing on Haiden's grave."

Like a ghost or a shapeshifter, morphing into someone he wasn't.

And then dancing on his grave.

A shiver ran across her shoulders, and she shuddered.

"I wish I'd got to meet your Haiden," she said. "I'm sorry I didn't realise something was wrong sooner."

"It's not your fault. Filip Nilsson was an accomplished liar and manipulator. You weren't the first woman to be taken in by him."

The previous deaths the inspector had referred to had all been women. It seemed he made a habit of making women believe he was something he was not, and then killing them when the women found out. The police had been on his tail, and he'd realised he had to get out of the country.

Just like her, Haiden Lindgren had been in the wrong place at the wrong time. Filip had seen how much alike they'd looked, and then discovered his plans to go to the UK to study. He'd killed Haiden and stolen his ID shortly before the coach had left, and simply picked up Haiden's bag, including his mobile phone, and boarded the coach as Haiden Lindgren. He'd been lucky that no one on the coach had met him before or that his parents hadn't seen him off at the station.

"I wish we'd driven him to the coach," Hugo admitted. "But he was twenty-three years old and always was independent. If we'd driven him there, he'd still be alive today, and you wouldn't have gone through everything you did."

So, they didn't hate her, or blame her for what had happened. They were blaming themselves as much as she'd been blaming herself.

"It's not your fault," she said, laying her hand on Hugo's arm.

Violet shook her head. "Only Filip Nilsson is to blame."

Yes, Filip Nilsson. Not Haiden Lindgren. Haiden Lindgren was dead, and these were his grieving parents. She'd never known Haiden. The only man she'd ever known was Filip, and she doubted she'd ever really known the real him. He probably hadn't even known who he was himself, by the end.

Maybe she could finally make peace with that.

Kristen hugged Haiden's parents goodbye, and they thanked her again, though she could never truly accept gratitude for killing a man.

Then she took her sister's hand and walked away from the grave, finally leaving Haiden Lindgren and Filip Nilsson behind her.

About the Author

M.K. Farrar is the pen name for a USA Today Bestselling author of more than thirty novels. 'Some They Lie' is her first psychological thriller, but won't be her last. When she's not writing, M.K. is rescuing animals from far off places, binge watching shows on Netflix, or reading. She lives in the English countryside with her husband, three daughters, and menagerie of pets.

You can sign up to MK's newsletter here at her website www.mkfarrar.com[1] or check out her facebook page, https://www.facebook.com/MKFarrar.

She can also be emailed at mkfarrar@hotmail.com. She loves to hear from readers!

Also by the Author

<u>SOME THEY LIE</u>[1]

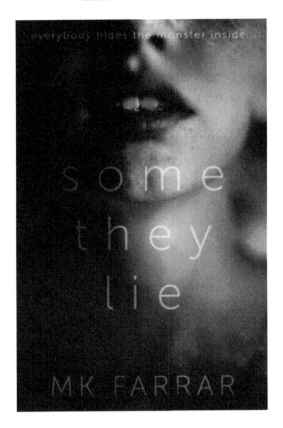

Everybody hides the monster inside...

When **Olivia Midhurst** meets Michael, she doesn't fool herself that he's the perfect guy. No one is perfect—she knows that better than most. Everyone has their **secrets**.

But something about Michael's behaviour sets her nerves on edge, and, when people around her start to go **missing**, and then turn up **dead**, she's forced to act.

Knowing the police will never believe what she's witnessed, and terrified her accusations will only drag up the past she's worked so hard to **bury**, Olivia has no choice but to take things into her own hands...

*Get this new, **heart-racing, psychological thriller** from Amazon[2] today!*

IN THE WOODS[3]

Death is easy. Surviving... can be murder.
Twenty-three year old Cassandra Draper is the latest **victim** of
the **serial killer** police have dubbed 'The Magician', due to his
ability to make women disappear.
Abducted and drugged, he takes her out into the middle of
nowhere, where he chains her to a tree trunk.

---

3. https://www.amazon.com/dp/B07T63GK1K

She thinks things can't get any worse, but a freak accident renders her completely **alone**.

And no one knows where she is.

She thought being **abducted** by a serial killer was as bad as things could get....

But she's about to learn there are worse things than being dead.

*Order this **edge-of-your-seat thriller** from **Amazon**[4] today!*

Dedication

I always say writing a book is a solitary process, and yet so many people are involved when it comes to the final production. I couldn't do my job without them. First of all, I want to thank my long-time editor, Lori Whitwam. We've worked together for years now, and she never lets me down. Thanks to my proofreaders—Tammy Payne from Book Nook Nuts, my long time reader, Linda Helme, and my mum, Glynis Elliott—I finally wrote another book you could read!

Thank you to the cover designers, the talented folks over at Deranged Doctor Design. I spotted this cover as a pre-made over a year ago, and snapped it up before this book was much more than an idea. Final thanks to K.A Richardson, for allowing me to grill her on police procedural for this book. Any mistakes that have been made are purely down to me and my need for a little creative writing! K.A. is an author, too, so make sure you go and check out her books.

And of course, huge thanks to you, the reader, for taking the time to read my work. I hope you've enjoyed the book and will hurry on over to Amazon to check out my other psychological thrillers, *Some They Lie* and *In the Woods*.

Until next time!

M K Farrar

Printed in Great Britain
by Amazon